I0591323

The Bachelor in
SPACE

LEIGH WYNDFIELD

OMNIfic PUBLISHING

LOS ANGELES

Omnific Publishing
2355 Westwood Blvd., Suite 506
Los Angeles, CA 90064
www.omnificpublishing.com

First Omnific eBook edition, January 2022
First Omnific trade paperback edition, January 2022

The characters and events in this book are fictitious. Any similarity to real persons, living or dead, is coincidental and not intended by the author.

Library of Congress Cataloguing-in-Publication Data

Wyndfield, Leigh.
The Bachelor in Space / Leigh Wyndfield – 1st ed. ISBN: 978-1-623422-72-1
1. Contemporary Romance — Fiction. 2. Space — Fiction.
3. Science Fiction — Fiction. 4. Humor — Fiction. I. Title

10 9 8 7 6 5 4 3 2 1

Cover Design by Sweet n' Spicy Designs
Interior Book Design by Amit Dey
Printed in the United States of America

CHAPTER ONE

*L*ynette Smith stepped from the shuttle into the dilapidated landing hangar on the Space Station Genesis III with a feeling of impending doom.

Taking in her surroundings with a quick glance, she realized that despite being hailed as the next destination in luxurious adventure travel, this old, previously abandoned space station was long overdue for basic maintenance. Wires hung willy nilly from opened panels and the bare metal walls of the hangar, which had once been hunter green, were now gouged and marred. Reality TV was about lush optics and exotic locations. This looked like the inside of a tin can that had been filled with rocks and rolled down a long hill.

She should never have let Hank Carson talk her into this.

"Hank," she said, resisting the urge to turn around and walk right back onto the shuttle they'd arrived in. She wasn't a dramatic person, didn't as a rule ever throw her hands wide to emphasize a point or stomp off in a rage. But in this moment, she wanted to scream her disappointment, with curse words thrown in for emphasis.

There were other reality TV shows begging to hire her and she could have taken a pass on this gig. But as usual when it came to Hank, she opened her mouth to say no and ended up saying yes instead. As a consolation prize to her stupidity, she'd won everything she'd wanted in contract negotiations. Mainly because she had the ultimate leverage. For the first time in her TV career, she didn't want the job.

Beside her, Hank stared at the wires and mumbled something she thought might have been, "this wasn't in the brochure." The puzzled, slightly worried expression only made him more handsome, the lowered brows and pursed lips adorable. His blond hair, green eyes and tall, lithe runner's body might be the perfect package, but it was his mind that made him dangerous.

She feared she might grow to hate him before this was all over.

The only new thing in the entire hangar was an axe someone had affixed to the wall, the steel blade shining in the dim lighting. She didn't even want to know why it was there. It would be their luck if it was supposed to be used to fight off invading aliens.

"What a dump," Russ said, summarizing her thoughts as he joined them. Russ had been one of her contract demands because he was the best cameraman in the business. If anyone could produce good film from this lemon, it was him. He'd been getting in shape lately, both thinning down and bulking up, thanks to cutting out caffeine drinks when he wasn't on a shoot and throwing around the iron at the gym. Lynette wondered what he'd look like without the ever-present partial beard, which made him look sloppy instead of ruggedly handsome as it did for some men.

"Let's not judge too quickly," Hank said.

She knew Hank thought Genesis III was going to be his biggest coup yet on his quest to bring the far reaches of the universe to reality TV. While a series of missteps, a crazy man, and an alien craft had cut short their filming on Mars, Hank planned to right his past wrong by going back into space. The owner of the space station, Milton Banks, had given them a sweet deal to film here, hoping the publicity would make this a destination spot for weddings and other events.

They had two days before the cast arrived to get everything set up to shoot the final three episodes. This should have been a piece of cake. But hope died as she watched an old, dilapidated Scantron droid unloading their supplies, pausing as some sort of malfunction made it sputter, then lurching forward to add another box in a stack.

"Well," Hank began, studying the damaged walls.

She paused to hear the spin he'd put on this trash heap, although how he would defend this, she was interested to hear.

"We can spruce up the place, hang some curtains—"

"Hello! Hello!" an older, white-haired man shouted from a nearby open hatch, his voice ricocheting around the small hangar. He came forward with his hand out and grasped Hank's from where it still hung limply at his side, pumping up and down with more energy than expected from someone his age. His white hair and portly structure testified to the fact he was a man of hearty appetites and enthusiasm, the beige suit reminiscent of salesmen of old. "I'm Milton Banks, owner and proprietor of Genesis III!" His sentences were spoken with big, fat exclamation marks at the end.

Hank opened his mouth to respond, but Milton cut him off.

"Well, let's not stand around here," he said, looking scornfully at the rogue wiring, as if it was the wiring's fault it wasn't cared for. "Come with me to the circus." He pulled Hank down a similarly beat-up hall at a quick stroll.

Hank followed with obvious reluctance, most likely, warry of the complications ahead, Russ hot on his heels. "What's the circus?" he asked, finally getting a word in edgewise.

"It's the center of the station. You'll find it's the answer to all your dreams," Milton said, as if he were an announcer in the center ring.

"If the wiring is this bad, I'm going to have trouble with the cameras," Russ mumbled scornfully to Lynette, but what he really meant was *you hauled me here. This is your fault.*

Russ might not be perfect, but he was the best reality TV cameraman in the business and he never missed perfect shots. If two contestants were smashed in a closet at four in the morning conspiring against one of the other women, Russ was there. He didn't sleep. He didn't leave his bank of computers except to hold a camera in an action shot. She didn't think he even went to the bathroom, although how he could hold that many energy drinks in his bladder was a mystery. Usually, he had a staff of flunkies working for him, but he'd reluctantly agreed to come up here alone.

For her. And look what she'd done to them both.

"Think of it as your biggest challenge. Nothing defeats you, Russ," she said with forced cheeriness. Because unless they ran back to the shuttle and chained themselves there, it was too late to go back now.

Russ preened a bit, but his generally morose personality made him add, "You can't get blood from a stone."

No, you couldn't. So why was she here?

Because there was a part of her, a part she wished she could excise from her life, that would follow Hank Carson anywhere.

Although this time, she'd almost beaten it down. Almost.

As a realist, Lynette knew there was no chance for her romantically with Hank, despite the fact she occasionally felt a spark of some kind flare between them. Hank liked his women tall and thin, perfectly turned out, with the symmetrical facial features God rarely bestowed. And while Lynette judged her looks to be girl-next-door pretty, she wasn't in that league, with ten extra pounds that refused to go away for longer than brief periods, a five-foot-four frame, and mouse brown hair that wouldn't do much of anything but go into a ponytail. Which was fine. She liked herself and didn't want to be anything other than what she was. But she wasn't naïve enough to think that Hank would pick someone like her, even if they did work together like peanut butter and jelly.

She watched her boss as Milton pulled him along, the casual jeans and long-sleeved t-shirt a rare outfit for Hank who preferred sleek power suits and expensive shoes. His blond hair was cut short for those moments he had to charm the executive producers out of their money.

Charming was his middle name, but as an old reality TV pro, Lynette wasn't easily charmed. He respected her ability to do her job, she knew, but he expected her to do miracles without the proper tools and he'd run roughshod over her if she let him. She doubled her personal vow to never be charmed by him again. She was a kick-ass woman who wasn't going to let this mission fail. Her career depended on it.

Lynette stopped herself from touching a nearby hanging wire, afraid it might shock her.

"You think he can pull this off?" Russ asked, filming their trip down the hall, because Russ filmed everything.

"I'm not sure," she admitted, wondering if Hank had finally met his match. This place was supposed to have three opulent suites that would wow the viewing audience. She couldn't imagine what they must look like. She pictured a dive motel she'd once found her best key grip in when he'd gone on a bender and prayed things wouldn't be that bad.

Then they passed out of the hall into the top floor of the circus, a three-story tall hub that accessed the rest of the station.

Everyone stopped.

"Wow," Russ said, echoing her thoughts.

"As you can see," Milton babbled, "I've changed the color scheme to give it some pop." He pointed to the faux pink marble on the column supporting the spiral staircase and the flamboyant turquoise blue on the walls. "Must have a place for brides to make an entrance."

Where the hall had been a falling-apart mess, she had to admit this room was amazing, certainly the perfect location for a dramatic entrance.

Lynette tried to picture herself wearing a poofy white confection walking down the steps, but just couldn't get there. Her work on what she often thought of as *LoveTV* had made her pretty pessimistic. There weren't too many couples still together past the four hundred days they agreed to in their contracts. That took them to the next season's last episode, where they were required to take the audience through their (rented) homes and gush about how awesome it was to have found *the one* before they could quietly walk away from each other. Still, if you ended up with someone who was fun, staying in a mansion for a year living a dashing lifestyle could be amazing.

Not that the show hadn't had real love matches. They had. They just didn't have that many. It was rare, which she supposed was why so many people coveted love so badly.

While she didn't understand the desire to compete for a husband, she found she could only do her job if she didn't judge the contestants for their choices. What she did understand was wanting love. She wanted it. Didn't everyone? But instead of an opulent lifestyle, Lynette's goals went more toward drinking coffee on a lazy Saturday while she and the man she loved read the news to each other off their tablets.

"We'll introduce them one by one as they come down the stairs." Hank flowed down the stairs in a perfect parody of a woman gliding on high heels. "We can give their deets as they make the journey, then for the two who are voted off, we'll have them climb back up." He turned, dropped his shoulders in defeat and mimicked the walk of shame to rejoin them.

Lynette couldn't help but grin. Beside her Russ filmed it all, probably for his post-show blooper reel, which Lynette had to admit was always a highlight of every show.

Staring down three stories, she was surprised to see the middle of the room taken up by a bar, complete with several couples that would take the shuttle she'd just arrived in home. They appeared to be enjoying cocktails, even though it was early in the morning. Silver overstuffed chairs, small side tables on which sat vases with what appeared to be real red roses, and a grand piano in one corner completed the decor. How the hell they had gotten all this stuff here, she didn't know.

Reality TV in space was filled with challenges. The contestants couldn't have the most romantic dates imaginable trapped in a tiny, far away location. Famous rock stars weren't about to magically walk through a door and serenade the bachelor and his chosen dinner date. There were no moments in hot air balloons with romantic kisses as the camera zoomed out to show the amazing backdrop. Having group dates in space was almost impossible because of the small room sizes.

Lynette knew she'd spend most of her time lion taming bored contestants that couldn't lay out by the pool working on their tan, or obsessively running on the treadmill in the gym, or any of the regular things they did to keep themselves entertained and only mildly unhappy. Lynette did have a couple activities planned, but the lack of room was truly the main issue up here. Besides, even as amazing as she was at her job, she wasn't Jesus or Bewitched's Samantha Stephens. She couldn't turn wine into water with a twitch of her nose.

The tour began in earnest from there. "The station started as an international project with over twenty nations taking turns living here. Each of them expanded the facilities, adding new sections and upgrading the technology. Sadly, when longer-range ships were invented, Genesis III fell out of fashion and was abandoned." Milton pulled them along, chatting and waving. "The station is divided into two sections across three floors. We call them north and south, although directions mean nothing up here. North will be open to you and your film crew. I'm afraid anything to the south will be off limits." Milton grinned as he hustled them down the third-floor north wing. "Think of the south side as behind the curtain in the Land of Oz." He chuckled as if the metaphor delighted him.

Lynette was sure he hadn't bothered to upgrade the south side of the station. It quickly became apparent that Milton hadn't spent a dime anywhere he didn't think he had to. Gorgeous rooms led into broken-down hovels, even on the good north side.

"Film around it!" Milton gave a flamboyant wave to toss aside any concerns at the ramshackle places.

Lynette figured they could, but they would have to put cameras in the bad areas too, or else the women would take their cat fights there. Most rational women didn't want to be caught on TV acting like crazy people. She understood the inclination to try to hide bad behavior, but if the contestants wanted anonymity, they shouldn't have signed away their privacy to come on the show.

She peered into the smallest bathroom she'd ever seen, a box that had a toilet, with a showerhead above it, making the most of the space. The thought of showering here made her glad they'd only be staying a week.

"They won't be fighting in here," Russ declared with some satisfaction over her shoulder. Russ wanted a minder stationed in every bathroom to make sure women couldn't sneak around. Ethically, he couldn't film in the bathroom, but after Hank had nixed the extra staff, he'd formulated a plan to put microphones in all spaces a person could squeeze two bodies into.

"Nope," she agreed, knowing he would figure out where they would fight.

Conflict brought viewers, viewers brought sponsors, sponsors paid for filming. While she wished they could sell only love, the fact was, without the cat fights, they would never have the money to film.

Behind her, Milton was giving Hank a rundown on how he thought they should set up their shoots, Hank nodding in agreement. But Lynette knew Hank would only do what was in the contract, no more and no less. And the contract wouldn't have said where they could and couldn't film, because they had to film everywhere to get their best footage.

"This is tight," Hank said, replacing Russ in the doorway, blocking her in. "Nobody will be sneaking in here for sex."

"Oh, I don't know," she said, studying the space. "Where there is a will, there is a way." She meant it as a joke, but a couple crazy positions flashed through her mind. A vision of a strong, muscled male back reflected in the mirror filled her head and she found the idea of having sex here not as repugnant as it should have been.

"I guess they could leverage the wall. Maybe someone could put their ass on the sink." Hank stepped inside to get a feel for the tight area, making her shrink back between the wall and the toilet's edge, but his clothing brushed hers.

And for possibly the first time since they started working together, he moved into her personal space. He wasn't currently touching her, but he was firmly into her zone. Suddenly, the male back she saw in her mind's eye was no longer anonymous, but instead belonged to the man next to her.

The air shifted and he met her gaze, his forest green eyes puzzled. Amusement faded from their faces, and she realized the talk of sex had led to thoughts of sex for him as well.

And she knew, beyond a shadow of a doubt, that they could have sex in this bathroom without any trouble at all. His smell, a combination of cinnamon and spicy male, curled around her, and her heart pounded, as if the air had grown thin.

She could have sex with Hank without a second thought, right here in this tight room, gasping for breath as he rammed deep. She shivered, the thought so crystal clear and vivid, she could almost feel him inside her.

Hank's eyes narrowed and he leaned toward her, slowly, as if he fought it. She felt her eyes widen and a hand rose to his chest but not to stop him, maybe to pull him closer. She wasn't sure. Her mind had stopped functioning, stuttering on the thought that Hank Carson is going to kiss me.

"Did you see this?" Russ said excitedly from a million miles away in the next room.

Hank jerked back as if he'd been slapped, blinking at her, the spell dissolving.

Lynette heaved in a breath, fighting to find her mind, which seemed to have gone away, possibly to Earth where she wished she was currently. Instead of sanity, she got a head full of his scent. Sandalwood, she decided, and cinnamon. It made her dizzy with the need to lean in for more.

You are NOT going to have sex with Hank Carson. If word gets out, you'll never work a TV show again. Your name will be raked through the mud and everyone will laugh at you.

Hank could get away with it, but the woman never could. A small voice said Hank was enough of a stand-up guy, he'd never tell anyone. But that way lay dragons. Everyone knew two people could keep a secret only if one of them was dead.

Besides, even if he didn't tell, it would ruin their working relationship for all time, and he had promised his support pitching her idea for a new show. She wasn't going to screw up her career for a screw in a miniscule bathroom, even if it had the potential to be amazing.

She hoped this wasn't a sign she was losing her mind.

CHAPTER TWO

*H*ank nodded at something Milton said but had no idea what it was, as the older man showed them the next two suites, pattering on about how much money he'd spent doing the upgrades to turn Genesis III into a world-class hotel in space.

A piece of wire tangled in his hair. He brushed it away and caught a slight tremor in his fingers.

What the fuck had just happened? He'd almost kissed Lynette. Not only kissed, but he knew if they'd been alone, he would have had her right there on the sink in the tiny bathroom if she'd agreed. He'd seen the scene in his mind. First, he'd strip off her shirt, bury his head between her breasts and taste his way downward to the edge of her jeans. What had started out as a joke had turned into something else entirely.

Jesus.

With an act of extreme will, he managed to cool his raging desire and shift his fading erection so it wasn't quite so obvious. Thank God he was in sturdy jeans and not dress slacks. He was lucky the whole thing hadn't ended up in the blooper reel.

Get a grip on yourself, Carson.

He'd staked his career on this show. In the never-ending challenge of one-upping not only his competitors' shows but his last creation, he had to make each Bachelor season better than the last. By taking the Bachelor into space, he was bringing TV to a whole different level. This was an Emmy in the making, he could feel it, the ultimate goal he'd had since the beginning of his career. It was the one thing he couldn't seem to accomplish, although he'd come close twice before.

He wasn't about to risk everything on a momentary loss of reason.

With Lynette.

It wasn't that he didn't like Lynette. He did. She was the best wrangler in the business. Smart, quick witted, and wise, even-tempered when confronted with the worst moments of humanity—her list of positives could fill a book. He would be totally screwed without her. And he'd always liked her, considered her a friend if he had to put a name to his feelings for her. There was no one else he wanted at his back more than he wanted her.

But this little twist, this momentary lapse of judgement on his part in the miniscule bathroom took him by surprise. This was the fifth show she'd worked for him and the eighth show they'd been on together. And he'd never once had a moment of lust with her, let alone a full-blown fantasy that had been so visceral, it had him leaning down to kiss her, his hands reaching to slide up her shirt.

"This," said Milton, his back to the next door as if to stop a stampeding horde from entering, "is my pièce de résistance." The older man's whole body thrummed with excitement. Whatever was behind the door was something he very much wanted them to be excited about.

Hank suppressed a sigh. Milton's station was less than he'd hoped for, but good enough. They could and would work with the hand they'd been dealt. He'd made a garbage heap of a hotel into a palace in Turkey three years ago. He could make this place shine. While he naturally saw the best in every situation, Hank had already noticed several potential challenges, but nothing he wasn't up to tackling. With Russ and Lynette at his side, he had no doubt he would knock this shoot out of the park.

Which is another reason you shouldn't follow through on the stab of lust you felt.

This was not the time to be distracted. He'd long ago made peace with the fact his mistress was his career, the thing he put his heart into.

Milton opened the door with a flourish to reveal... a hot tub.

Steam billowed up in a cloud, the tiny room barely allowing them to inch inside.

Lynette skirted the hot tub on the side away from him, all business as she studied the room. The moment between them was obviously a thing of the past for her. Good. It would be awkward if she was still thinking about it.

Like he was.

"We can work with this," Lynette said, studying the walls, which featured a port hole that showed outer space. Her back to him, she peered into the starry abyss. "Russ?"

He felt a little stung she hadn't asked him first, then shoved the thought aside. They weren't dating. Plus, Russ was in charge of the filming.

"Yeah, this will work," Russ said in his usual monotone. "I can place three cameras to cover every angle, but we'll keep space behind them for the kissing."

And Hank had the sudden vision of he and Lynette in the hot tub, making out with the stars behind them. Need he'd only just repressed roared back through his body.

What was going on? He did not pant after Lynette. Sure, she was cute and she had a fantastic laugh, but really, what the hell? He had never been attracted to her.

Milton glanced at his wrist. "Oh! I need to get the guests onto the shuttle! I'll be back soon. Please meet me in the circus." He bustled off, leaving the three of them alone for the first time.

"He might have put lipstick on, but this wiring is still a pig," Russ said, pulling a screwdriver from his pocket and popping open a fuse box.

"All the upgrades seem to be on the surface. Although the hot tub is a great touch." Lynette wasn't looking at him when normally she would have been giving him serious side-eye at the very least for hauling her here. They were great at that kind of non-verbal communication. Which meant their weird moment had impacted her as well. Not good. Now that he thought of it, it would have been more in character for her to at least make a couple pointed remarks to him when she saw this place was a dump.

Well, he wasn't going to highlight the bad. It was time to start embracing what they had to work with. "It's a fantastic touch, actually. This will make great TV. Hot water, too much champagne…" He cupped a handful of steaming water and let it drain out. "Think we can run all three of them through here? Or would that be too redundant?"

Lynette stared out the viewport without meeting his gaze. "We may have to. Unless there are more hidden gems Milton hasn't showed us."

"I am going to need to start wiring immediately. You're putting each of the women into one of the suites?" Russ was out the door without waiting for an answer or to see if they were following, oblivious that something was askew in his and Lynette's relationship.

"About earlier," he began, figuring it was best to get it all out in the open.

"Forget it," she said with a finality that brooked no argument. "We need to concentrate on the show."

"Absolutely," he said, more relieved than he wanted to admit, even to himself. He bowed for her to exit the room first.

She raised one eyebrow, as if this behavior puzzled her.

The little insult rankled. He had always been a gentleman. Although now that he considered it, he supposed he treated Lynette as one of the guys. He couldn't remember ever letting her leave a room first before.

She passed him with only a shake of her head, worry pulling her lips into a frown.

They trailed Russ back to the circus, which wasn't hard since every passage connected to the center of the station, to find Milton shepherding several couples to the landing hangar where they would return to Earth. They paused against the railing of the third floor to let the group climb the twisting staircase.

"This way, this way!" Milton's hands fluttered in an encouraging manner as he led the couples up.

Hank recognized an A-list movie star arm in arm with a woman who wasn't his wife leading the group. Maybe they were checking off a bucket list item.

Milton had approached Hank, offering an at-cost arrangement. Hank had spent a couple months thinking it over. He hadn't decided to go back into space lightly. Mars Bachelor had almost killed his sister the last trip, and while Margo was a pain in his butt most of the time, he loved her dearly. He wasn't planning to have anything go wrong this time and had thought he'd done his due diligence to guarantee that. There wouldn't be any alien space ships in this old station. But he hadn't counted on the condition of the station being an issue.

"Why the hell would anyone come here if they weren't working?" Russ asked, bewildered.

"Just to say they've done it," Lynette answered, leaning on the railing that ringed the three-story drop below them.

The couples and Milton climbed the circular stairs while Milton acted the tour guide, encouraging the woman who followed closely behind him to make sure she told all her friends about her experience. She assured him she would, tittering at Milton's jokes and loving his lavish attention.

Having paid for plenty of women's clothing, Hank could tell her smart jacket and Jimmy Choos alone had cost her what most people made in a month. When you had that kind of money, a quick trip into space wouldn't set you back at all.

Would he come here? He debated, thinking of the hot tub with the billion-dollar star view.

No, because he was always working.

But if he wasn't working?

Hank tried to picture it, but he'd spent the last fifteen years either prepping for a shoot, shooting, or making the rounds to get the money to make another show. Rinse. Repeat. And he loved it. All of it. He'd married his job and it was a perfect union. Not many people could say they were doing what they loved, but he could.

Although lately, he'd become mildly discontent. Just a niggle of unhappiness that wasn't like him. As if he wanted more from his life. Which was ridiculous, since he had everything he'd ever wanted. Except an Emmy.

Maybe it was too many Bachelor shows. Maybe he needed a switch. He'd been thinking about something more like a docu-series. Something like following cops around or maybe firefighters, although they rarely fought fires any longer since houses and furniture were built to be flame resistant, so that was out. Maybe he could do a docu-series on Milton's struggles to run an old space station as a luxury hotel? He went through a quick mental exercise to see if he could pull that off while they were here. Two shows for the price of one. He could almost imagine it.

Maybe after they wrapped the bachelor footage, he'd peek at what was left. He should have Lynette interview Milton. Or if he had time, he'd do it tonight. Sell it to Milton as more free advertising.

As always, the thought of a new project revved him up and a surge of adrenaline raced through his veins.

The rich people left down the beat-up old hallway, not seeming to give the battered paint a second glance.

"Let's check out the bar," Lynette suggested.

They began the long trek down the spiral staircase to the bottom where a lounge area took up the floorspace. The bar was a small, chest height six-seater with room for people to stand between the high stools bolted to the floor. A set of shelves held liquor bottles, which on closer inspection were actually secured individually to the wall. Everything was ringed with multicolored lights, the mirror behind it amplifying the display.

A robot, who had been standing still and dead, popped to life as they approached. Lynette jumped back as the robot's hands flailed.

"Welcome to Genesis III! I'm your bartender Alphie. What can I get for you?" The robot only had a body from the waist up, the lower half was a pole that ran back and forth along a track behind the bar. He was built to look like a cartoon of a man, with extra big, turquoise eyes and a permanent smile painted around a hole where his voice spilled forth. He blinked innocently, waiting obediently for their orders, his body clothed in a black tux jacket and crisp white shirt, with a dapper red bow tie.

Robots were out of favor back on Earth after some of the first prototypes had outlearned their makers and took over computer systems. Malfunctions of this type were the rule rather than the exception and legislation had been installed to outlaw all advanced intelligence robots. But Hank supposed Earth law wasn't enforced here. He'd never seen a working AI robot up close.

"Orange juice," Russ said, and for once, his face was lit with excitement.

"Coming right up," Alphie chirped, zooming along his track to a small fridge behind the bar.

"This is one of the old XRJ's. I thought they'd all been mothballed." Russ' excitement made his normally morose face into an animated mask of joy. He looked like a different person. For the first time, Hank noticed his cameraman had lost some weight since their last job together.

Alphie's tux lapels flapped as he bent down, clicked open a refrigerator and drew out a box of juice.

"They were all supposed to be," Lynette said, staring at Alphie as if he were a snake in the grass.

Hank found it interesting that he alone wasn't stirred up in some way by the addition of the robot. His only concern was the impact to the show and he was sure there wouldn't be one.

Russ, never one to understand people's subtler emotions, still managed to hear the negativity in her voice. "Don't be like that, Lynette. These guys aren't going to take over the world. He probably isn't even attached to the ship's computer system."

Alphie put a small napkin on the bar, then carefully placed a glass of orange juice exactly in the middle. "I am sorry to say that you are incorrect. I am fully integrated with the ship's system." He smiled happily at Russ, waving a little to indicate his drink was ready.

"Great," Lynette said, her usually upbeat tone turning grumpy.

"Let's not get caught up in insignificant details," Hank said, trying to head off her dip into the negative. After all, what did it matter if the bartender robot was attached to the ship's computer?

"When we end up dealing with a rogue robot taking over the ship, I'm going to quote you," she warned, but a reluctant smile battled on her lips.

"May I get you something?" Alphie asked her, sounding hopeful.

"No."

The robot's shoulders dramatically slumped in disappointment.

She turned away to study the bottom of the circus. "We'll keep the women here, I think, for at least some shoots. This space will film well." But even as she complimented it, she stared dubiously at the pink faux-marble columns.

"I see you found the bar," Milton called from above. He hustled down the stairs, spry for his age and weight.

Lynette sighed, clearly thinking Milton was an issue.

And maybe she was right. She had a knack for anticipating problems.

Hank liked Milton, but then again, he liked most people. He couldn't help himself. People appealed to him on a basic level. If he was super honest with himself, which he preferred not to be, he really only liked people on a superficial level. He could meet people all day long and leave feeling energized, but one hard conversation with a woman he was dating and he felt like he'd been hit with a hammer. Deep relationships were hard and he liked living an easy life.

A rumble shook the station, starting as a silent tremor, but rapidly growing louder.

"What the hell?" Hank asked, grabbing the bar to steady himself.

Russ tossed back the orange juice in one swig, clearly preparing for mayhem.

The bottles rattled in their fixtures, adding to the growing noise.

"No need to worry," Alphie said, his smile still in place.

Hank wasn't reassured.

"Alphie is quite right!" Milton said, out of breath as he double-timed the last bit of winding staircase. "There is no need to worry. It's simply that the shuttle is taking off."

The rattling grew more intense. "This can't be good," Lynette said and Hank steadied her when she rocked backwards.

"No need to worry," Alphie repeated happily.

"It's just temporary," Milton called as he hoofed it the last few steps to the bar, puffing for air, keeping a firm hand on the railing.

"This happens every time a shuttle departs?" Hank asked, disbelieving. He felt his teeth rattle in his head.

"Yes, but guests are never here for this part." Milton seemed a bit defensive for the first time, his friendly face crunched into a frown. "You're seeing some of the behind-the-scenes that allow for the magic." He said the last word with a flourish.

The rumble died down as if on cue, all the bottles rattling to a standstill.

"I guess so," Lynette said, and Hank could tell she'd decided to smooth over the small rift.

Then the lights went out, leaving them in darkness for a heartbeat, just long enough for Hank to think *oh shit*.

Alphie flopped forward, his head bouncing twice on the bar top.

The emergency lighting clicked on with a snap, putting the bar into half-darkness.

"Is this normal?" Lynette asked.

"Oh yes, totally normal," Milton said hastily. "I'll be back in one moment." He turned and ran back up one flight of stairs, then raced along the railing to the right into the forbidden south zone, where he disappeared down a long corridor.

"I think maybe Alphie was wrong," Hank said mildly, because it seemed there was reason to worry.

"Of course he was wrong. He's not a thinking being." Lynette marched toward the stairs.

"Where are you going?"

"Do you think Milton is capable of handling this on his own?" Lynette asked, double-timing it up the stairs.

She had a point.

He followed her, conscious of Russ filming them as he trailed behind.

"He has a staff, surely," Hank said, not as sure as he should be, but figuring there had to be an upside here. Despite his naturally positive outlook, even he could admit this wasn't a great start. And Hank had a bad feeling Milton had lied when he said losing power was normal. There had been something on his face.

But surely Milton wasn't on this station with only old robots for assistance?

When they finally located their host, he was standing in a room that must be the working hub of the station. In the half-light, Hank could see the huge bank of computers on the left glowing weakly. The right was a mass of wires, which terminated into a large metal box that took up most of the room.

"Jackson, I need to know if you can get it up and running. We need power. Now." Milton voice trembled a bit as he spoke to someone hidden by the large box.

"Go away, Milton. I can't think when you're hovering," a male voice growled.

"Please tell me you have a way for us to get the power restored?" Lynette asked, while Russ entered the room and drifted to the side for a better shot.

"You can't be here." Milton charged forward, his hands waving to shoo them out. "This is an employee-only area."

"I think we need some answers, before the cast arrives."

Milton's face hardened. "Please stay at the bar until I update you further."

The man behind the metal box stood up, all six and a half feet of him. His long blond hair was held back in a ponytail and his t-shirt strained across broad, muscled shoulders. Standing in a pool of green half-light, he glowed, the wrench in his hand glinting like Thor's hammer.

"Wow," Lynette breathed, her eyes huge. "He's a Greek God."

"What?" Hank asked, doing a double take as Lynette appeared to drool at the view. He wasn't used to Lynette looking at anyone like that, except maybe—he paused wondering if this was true or just his own ego talking—when she stared at him.

Milton kept coming, arms windshield wipering in his panic, saying, "This will all be taken care of in a few moments." Sweat was soaking through his suit jacket at the armpits as he approached, making Hank back away. Lest their bodies touch.

"You might need our help," Hank suggested, although he was a producer, not an electrician.

"I'm Lynette," she said, introducing herself to the man with the wrench in his hand.

Hank sidestepped to block Lynette's view of Jackson, for some reason more concerned about this new development than the fact they seemed to be floating in space without power.

Milton herded them through the door. "I'll be down shortly with an update," he said, pushing the two of them into the hall, before firmly shutting the door in their faces.

CHAPTER THREE

"Who is that guy?" Lynette asked, wondering what impact the addition of a hunky man would do to an already volatile moment in the show. She'd seen the simple addition of a gardener in one show change the whole outlook of the women, and not for the better. Depending on his personality, Jackson could easily charm away anyone feeling unappreciated or those who thought they might be voted out next.

Hank seemed lost in his own head. "Should we leave?"

"What?" she asked, trying to switch subjects. "Leave where?"

"Here," he said, sounding irritated with her, but he was acting so un-Hank like she was having trouble following. "Go back to Earth."

She stared in amazement at Hank, who had never once backed down from any challenge. So many times, it had been she who argued to abandon a story line or location. Pleaded with him to please, for the love of good TV, go to a new hotel/town/ country.

"The next shuttle arrives in two days. We could simply join the contestants on the ship and return to Earth."

"You want to give up?" She was having trouble believing it. "Not that I don't agree. This place isn't what we were led to believe. My gut says we leave while we still can." Not that she really meant that. They could film here. It would just super suck.

"What am I thinking?" Hank rolled his shoulders as if to shrug off his out-of-character waffling. "We'll be fine."

"No wait. You were going in the right direction," she said, trying to bring him back around. "We could leave the boxes of equipment and walk away." It felt right. Escape while they could. There was nothing here they couldn't fake down on Earth.

But Hank was now shaking his head.

She tried again. "We can go to somewhere else and film. Morocco maybe. You've always said you wanted to film there."

"It's been done. The Bachelorette went there two seasons ago," he said, dismissing it.

She sighed, knowing the moment had passed.

The door opened again and Milton strong armed a still-filming Russ into the hall. The door banged shut, leaving them all staring at it in surprise.

Russ dropped his camera for once. "Milton has a bit of crazy in him I wasn't expecting."

"Yeah," Lynette agreed. "Hank was thinking about abandoning the project and going home on the next shuttle." She figured Russ of all people would agree that was a good idea.

"Really?" Russ studied Hank as if he were a new camera.

"Temporary insanity." Hank brushed it off.

"You aren't one to give up," Russ agreed.

"I'm not giving up. We're staying. Let's get the cameras in place."

"In the dark? How is that going to happen?" Lynette asked, annoyed that Hank had swung firmly in the other direction. No thanks to Russ, who hadn't reacted the way she'd thought he would. She'd expected a full litany of wiring complaints from him at the very least.

"Unknown." Russ was always one for brevity.

Lynette struggled with her already fraying temper. "We're burning through one of two days we have for set up. Coming early will end up being a complete waste if we can't get the cameras in place before they get here."

Hank rolled his shoulders again, irritating her.

She leaned into his space in annoyance. "I thought you didn't want a repeat of Mars Bachelor? Because I'm not having any more slip-ups."

Slip-ups like the one that had allowed Misty, one of the contestants from Mars Bachelor, to get a leg up (so to speak) on the competition. As head wrangler, Lynette knew that the secret to success for these shows was proper preparation. No mingling should ever be allowed that hadn't been carefully choreographed.

Hank had paired the bachelor, Chad Harper, with Misty, saving the show from sure ruin. Chad had slept with Misty on one of the first days, alienating every other woman on the show, and infuriating Lynette. It had been a clear violation of the rules. She'd wanted to fire Misty on the spot and make Chad pay for a breach of contract. But Hank, in a "love rules everything" moment only someone with his balls of steel could pull off, had the viewing audience swooning in joy when Chad chose Misty and refused to have anyone else. Well, it had been Hank's sister Margo's suggestion, but only Hank could make anything that crazy into one of the best show endings ever.

"I don't." He narrowed his eyes in annoyance for her bringing up the past.

"Then we'd better use every minute of the next two days to make this perfect. What can we do without electricity? Pick camera locations maybe? Lay out equipment? Assign rooms?" she asked, her voice rising.

"Aren't there only three of them? How long will it take to assign rooms?" Russ asked.

She stopped him from raising the camera. "Don't be a smart ass, Russ. I'm not in the mood." If they were going to stay, which she thought was a mistake, they needed to stop wasting the time they had left. "Let's go get those crates and distribute the cameras. If this dump ever gets the power back on, we need to be ready to spring into action."

Hank grabbed her arm as she marched by. "Listen, about this guy Jackson—"

"Focus, Hank. If you haven't noticed, we are in the middle of a crisis and need all hands on deck." She reversed the hold and took his hand instead, ignoring the little tingle that always came with his nearness. "You need to help us with these crates. I'll take care of Jackson later."

For some reason, Hank didn't look reassured.

Even in the half light, they worked their asses off. Lynette rode herd on both men, since Russ had a tendency to hyper-focus on weird trivialities and Hank kept wanting to talk about the maintenance man.

Who was hot. And would be a problem. But not a problem they needed to deal with today.

She pulled a trolley stacked with camera equipment along the hall to the second-floor suites, wondering if Hank was right to worry this much. They could ban Jackson from the contestants. In fact, she'd corner Milton and make sure he agreed to keep the maintenance guy as far away from filming as possible.

Resting for a brief moment in a long string of tasks, she kicked off the countdown timer in her mind. They had a little more than twenty-four hours remaining until the three contestants and the bachelor showed up.

After spending an amazing two months in Zanzibar, the bachelor had chosen the final three women, all of whom he had declared himself in love with.

This show's bachelor, Max Botta, was a Formula One driver who had that classic, clean handsomeness their viewers loved. And his three last ladies—Emma, Mima, and Kyla (who she'd begun to refer to in her own mind as the Three-A's since their names ended in that letter)—were each beautiful, smart, and filled with personality. Which their viewers also loved. Sometimes Lynette wondered if maybe adding some introverts into the mix wouldn't make better couples in the end. After all, Max had the personality of someone who liked to be in the limelight, and his personality might meld better with a partner who would let him shine.

On her to-do list were three romantic dinners and three overnight set ups, since filming would stop when the clothing came off. The next morning, she would interview each woman about how good in the sack the bachelor was. She could do that with her eyes closed. Or so she'd thought. She hadn't expected the station to be this grim.

The only thing that could go sideways was the bachelor being bad in bed. He had to have sex with three women in three straight days. While this might seem like every man's wet dream, the reality was most had performance anxiety at the very least. Luckily, the contestants often lied if they had a bad night, not wanting to be blamed if things went wrong. A sad, but true statement on the state of sexual relations in this supposedly advanced day and age.

This was the part of the show that icked her out if she thought about it, which she tried not to. She was a woman who wanted a man who only wanted her in bed. Upside down or sideways, the sex could go any direction as far as she was concerned. Lynette considered herself adventurous in bed. But she wasn't someone who shared. That was her line in the sand. Always. Working on the Bachelor had only cemented that she was a one-man woman.

More importantly, he better be a one-woman man.

She placed a crate in each of the three suites filled with some of the contestants' clothing and make-up. She would have dropped off the dress for tomorrow night's cocktail party as well, but she'd learned long ago only to give out one dress at a time for a myriad of reasons.

The suites were closer together than she'd like, with all three doors facing onto the same small piece of hall. The tight layout meant that the women who were left out would be tempted to meddle in the ongoing date. Lynette was paid to think these things through. She closed one of the suite doors and looked out the peephole to see Russ coming up the hall, looking ghostly in the eerie green half-light that lit his way.

Yep. She would have to remove the two other girls from the hall until after the bachelor and his date were firmly inside a suite, safe from 'accidentally' bumping into any of the others.

Russ went into the suite across the way, leaving the door propped open with his own trolley.

Lynette joined him. "This lighting is creeping me out."

"Yeah, it's very retro horror movie." Russ popped the fuse box hidden behind the bedroom door. The suites were tiny, but they had a seating area, a bedroom, and the tiny bath. Lynette studied the small love seat, trying to imagine the filming. If Russ had a handheld camera, he would be crowding the couple, making things awkward between the budding lovers. But sometimes the show needed that kind of shot.

"You know," Russ said from right behind her.

"Ack," she yeeped, grabbing her chest. She needed to calm down. But the green lighting reminded her of an alien movie she'd once seen, one where scary massive bug creatures were hiding in the shadows.

She reminded herself this wasn't that show.

Really, it wasn't.

No alien bugs would suck her juices out and then lay eggs in her body for their young to eat after hatching.

"I can hang these cameras, but if we don't get power back soon, I won't have time to do the wiring and catch a nap before filming," Russ said, not seeming to notice he'd scared the crap out of her. "That's going to make me grumpy."

"Okayyyy," she said, drawing out the ending since her first thought was that Russ was always grumpy.

"It's important I start fresh," he informed her, sounding for the first time like a prima donna. Russ never complained, always worked his ass off, and didn't make demands. These were the reasons she loved working with him. The fact he was going south on her wasn't a good sign.

She needed to refocus his attention. "Who are you? And what have you done with Russ?" she asked, hearing Hank's tread in the hallway.

"I'm being serious, Lynette." Russ did look genuinely put out.

"About what?" Hank asked.

She moved to get away from being too close to him, since their earlier loss of control made her nervous. This wasn't the time to make things worse. They were already in enough trouble without adding a budding lust-mance to it. "Russ is worried about his beauty sleep."

"What?" Hank asked, confused.

"I need a nap before filming begins." When Hank laughed, Russ added, "I'm being serious." He peered at them both closely. "Why are both of you acting so weird?"

"Okay," she said, briskly, going into full redirect mode. She'd dealt with harder cases than Russ with one eye closed. "If we end up without power much longer, why don't you take that nap now, instead of later?"

"A nap?" Hank asked, still confused.

"I'd rather sleep after I've got the cameras up. I don't want to spend the trip using a handheld." Russ shuddered as if that would be awful. And maybe it would be as bad for him as it would be for the cast members. Having Russ constantly right there would block the cast from dropping into the fantasy where they weren't really on a show, and things hadn't been contrived.

Hank shook his head, still lost. "What's the camera status?"

"All of them are distributed and ready for installation. If we have power, then we might get them up and running in time."

"Let's try not to be negative here—" Hank began.

"You don't even know what negative is," Lynette muttered, feeling annoyed that Hank had been ready to leave, then changed his mind.

The lights came on around them.

"See?" Hank spread his arms to encompass the station. "Positivity is the answer."

She felt like socking him right on that hot mouth of his. "Whatever." She stomped off to find Milton. They needed to have a pow-pow. Annoyingly, Hank trailed her, but he didn't try to force her into conversation as he usually did. Which was a good thing for him, because she wasn't in the mood.

They found Milton at the bar, talking to Alphie, who was making him what looked like a Manhattan.

"Little early for drinking isn't it?" Lynette asked, taking a quick look at her watch. Ten AM, but she supposed up here time had different meaning. Still, she would need to watch his drinking like a hawk. She found that when people started day drinking during a shoot they were one step away from staggering around, raging at the fates, and ugly crying over their past love lives.

"Mr. Banks always celebrates with a drink after the visitors leave," Alphie said in his peppy voice.

She ignored him. It. Robots didn't have genders. Instead, she gave Milton her laser serious look. "We're working at double time getting cameras up and will continue for the rest of the day and through the night."

"Of course, of course, just let me know how to help," Milton said, picking up his drink two handed to stop a slight tremor from sloshing liquid over the lip.

"I need your assurances that your handyman will stay far away from the contestants."

He swallowed and sighed in contentment, then blinked a couple times. "My handy-who?"

"Jackson?"

Beside her Hank frowned, a rare expression for him.

Milton chuckled. "Oh, he isn't the handyman. He's the space engineer."

Of course he was. That would only make him more attractive, not less.

"No matter who he is, he can't be exposed to the contestants. We have to maintain a pristine environment where the only men they meet are our staff and the bachelor." While Russ wasn't a potential trip-up since the contestants weren't around him long enough to see his finer points, Hank had caused more than one woman" to become distracted. Not that he ever encouraged them. Lynette had never seen Hank look twice at a contestant. Which was odd, now that she thought about it, since she was sure he could have any woman he put his focus on.

"Oh, I see what you mean." Milton took another slow sip, extra enjoying it. "Because he's a Prime Article."

Lynette noticed with even a couple of swallows, his hand tremor had stopped.

"A what?" Hank asked.

"Prime Article," Alphie said helpful as ever. "An 1800s slang word for the most beautiful person in the room. Although it was traditionally used for women, and I believe Jackson is a man."

Hank narrowed his eyes at the robot, which caused Lynette to feel unreasonably pleased that he was coming around to her side. Although Alphie wouldn't distract the contestants. Usually when filming, the support staff were almost all women, to cut down on possible mishaps.

"Exactly," Lynette agreed. "He needs to stay out of sight when they're around."

"Well, Jackson does what Jackson does. I'm afraid I have very little control over him." Milton took another careful sip, like a drunk who savors the beginning of their fall.

Lynette inhaled, wondering where her finesse skills had gone. "Aren't you the Commander of this space station?"

Milton straightened at the word Commander. "Well, yes, I guess I am."

"Then talk to him." She upped the ante. "Or would you like me to?"

"Maybe I should talk to him," Hank interrupted, something odd in his voice.

She narrowed her eyes. "Since when do you step on my role?" she asked in a surprised whisper. It better not have anything to do with the almost-kiss in the bathroom earlier, because she was already over it. Mostly. This was why she was a firm believer in not mixing business with pleasure. Men mistook a female's interest as a declaration of submission.

"No, no, I'll do it," Milton said hurriedly, ending the words by finishing the drink in one gulp.

"Okay," Lynette said, but she didn't feel reassured.

———

"Hey," Lynette whispered.

Hank's sleeping form stayed sleeping. Even in slumber, he was massively good looking, with a chiseled chin and thick eyelashes any woman would envy splayed across his cheeks. While he wasn't snoring, he was breathing deeply, attesting to his annoyingly perfect slumber.

Russ had crashed on the other side of what they were calling their command center, which had banks of monitors across a long table, two chairs and several racks filled with clothing and boxes of supplies. They'd also dragged in two futons they'd found in their explorations that rolled out to single beds.

She nudged his futon. "Hank." He'd asked her to wake him so his alarm wouldn't disturb Russ, who had wanted to sleep until the last minute.

He slept on. She'd had little sleep, tossing and turning as she thought about what it would have been like if his lips had actually touched hers.

Russ' snores filled the room, so loud she wondered if he had a medical condition. Then she remembered Russ wasn't one of her many worries.

"T-minus one hour until the contestants arrive," Lynette said loudly.

Nothing.

"Hank," she said, giving the futon a hard shove with her foot, not wanting to get too close to him.

"What?" he mumbled.

They'd worked their asses into the ground and separated to crash, although she'd laid awake with anxiety when her head hit the pillow. She'd debated visiting Alphie for some medicinal sleep help, but then she'd have to ask the robot for a favor, which she steadfastly wouldn't do. She knew it wasn't Alphie's fault other robots had ruined it for him, but she figured the wisest course was to stay away. Because even if he was supposed to not be sentient, humans had built something that wasn't quite human, but also wasn't fully metal either.

Hank's breathing evened back out again. He'd fallen back to sleep.

"Hank," she said louder.

No response.

She looked over at Russ, worried about waking him, but he snored on, oblivious.

"Hey!" she said sharply, clapping her hands twice right in his ear.

Hank gasped as if she'd thrown cold water on him. "I'm up I'm up I'm up, Jesus." Hank rolled to the edge of the futon, which dropped under his weight to spill him into the floor. He jerked away from the edge, barely catching himself.

"Feet on the floor," she ordered, something her mother had said all through high school.

"My god, you're evil in the mornings," he said, but he put his feet on the floor, which forced the rest of him into a sitting position.

"In the next hour, we have a ton to do, so let's get our game faces on," she said, trying for authoritative with a twist of peppy.

He offered his hand. "Help me up."

She stared at it, not wanting to touch him. Before the almost kiss (BAK as she'd referred to it in the depths of the night), she'd help him without hesitation. But now she wasn't sure any longer what her body was actually doing when it came to his pheromones. Or whatever the hell was going on here. But would it make things even more awkward if she refused? It might.

Against her better judgement, she took his hand, feeling the warm fuzzies creep up her arm.

Instead of barely using her help, he actually had her lifting him. She braced her feet and put her back into it, giving him a hearty pull. When he stood, he all of a sudden stopped relying on her. She staggered, stumbling toward the bank of equipment.

"Whoa now," he said, catching her arm before she crashed into the monitors.

And suddenly she was cradled in his arms, held tight to his chest, as if she were precious to him. Which she wasn't. She knew that. Their gazes were locked and her stomach tumbled as if she were in high school having her first kiss all over again.

Good lord. Get yourself together, Lynette!

She stared at his lips as they slowly lowered.

She should pull away. She should—

While she waffled, he completed the journey, their mouths pressing together, energy zinging down into her core.

Oh my God, she thought, her mind unable to think anything else at all. Oh my God, oh my God, oh my God.

She wanted this. So much. Her hand caught the back of his head to bring him closer.

Hank's touch was a whisper, barely sliding along her skin, the action causing her stomach to flip and her hand to shake where it held him.

This had been a secret wish she hadn't even admitted to herself. This had been something she had wanted, possibly for years.

Her whole world rocked and shifted, and her mind was caught in the thought that she could have him longer than this moment. They could go out on the sly. No one ever had to know. She could luxuriate in the feel of him, have down-and-dirty sex night after night. Keep things at work the same while they had a relationship they both could enjoy.

Because whatever she had with Hank Carson would not be long term. It would, at most, be a brief kind of fling, maybe a month, maybe two. That's how Hank rolled. He was a love 'em and leave 'em kind of guy.

She'd never had a fling before, but she was a strong, independent woman. She could have sex and not fall in love. She could.

Really, she could.

Hank deepened the kiss and her world shifted, his tongue running along her lips and then slipping in to touch hers. She gasped for breath, trembling with a need so great she wanted him right here, right now.

It was so amazing that it took her a moment to realize that her world was *literally* rocking.

Hank must have felt it too, because he broke away. She blinked several times to reengage her brain. The whole room vibrated and shivered.

"What's happening?" Hank asked, as confused as she was.

She had a quick thought that the station's duct tape had fallen apart and they were breaking into a million pieces, before a helpful voice came on the intercom.

"Looks like the shuttle is early, folks," a male voice said and from the deep, sexy purr, she realized it must be Jackson, because it sure wasn't Milton or Alphie.

She would need to talk to Milton, because adding to her growing list was that Jackson wasn't allowed to talk on the intercom. Ever. His voice said come hither you hot ladies and I will give you the night you've always wanted. That was asking for trouble.

"Crap." The contestants were here. She sprung forward to wake Russ. They needed the cameraman awake and functioning. "Russ!"

He snored on peacefully.

She didn't want to, but reluctantly she grabbed his foot and wiggled it. "Russ," she yelled.

The snoring stopped. "What?" he snapped, wide awake and grumpy as hell.

"The shuttle is landing."

"Shit," he said, but sat up.

She grabbed an energy drink from a box nearby and cracked it open, putting it in his hand. Then she left at a run. The hall jittered with the incoming shuttle. She had to be there to greet everyone and spring into action. Transitions were a crucial moment in the show, where everything could go to hell in a snap.

Sliding to a halt in the landing bay, she walked slowly onto the shuttle as if she had been waiting for them all along. First, she poked her head into the bachelor's room and told him she would disembark him after the ladies.

Then she went to find the women, who had been placed in a joint room with numerous cameras rolling to capture any moments.

"How was the trip?" she asked, going into her let's-get-excited persona she used to infuse energy into the group.

"Fatastic! It's like a dream come true," Mima said in the sing-song cadence of a contestant telling the cameras exactly what they wanted to hear. She bounced up, grabbing a huge purse that she slung over one shoulder.

The other two rose more slowly. From their closed, annoyed expressions, things must have gone sideways on the trip, and if she had to guess, Mima was to blame.

"What about you two? Enjoy the journey?" Lynette asked, trying to draw Kyla and Emma out of their ire. There was plenty of time for them to be mad at each other later.

"Yeah a dream come true," Kyla said, giving Mima the stink eye behind her back.

"I get motion sickness," Emma said. "But I can't wait to see Max again."

"This is going to be amazing. You are going to be blown away," Lynette said, trying to distract them from the exposed wiring and the peeling paint and hustle them into the circus as fast as possible.

All three gasped when they saw it and Lynette smiled, hoping Russ had the cameras set up to catch their awed expressions. This was what it was all about.

She herded them down one flight and along the hall toward their suites, answering a million questions from Mima alone. The black-haired beauty had some American Indian heritage in her past, based on her high cheekbones and gorgeous dark brown almond-shaped eyes. Lynette suspected the other two had stopped talking to her, based on Mima's frantic chatter.

When Lynette had come to the space station, she'd left the contestants in the care of the assistant wrangler, Sugar, who was a master when it came to being the heavy, complete with a major side of bitch. In real life, Sugar was the nicest person Lynette had ever met, but when she played Wrangler (with a capital W), she was an immovable force. Lynette loved her and wished she were here. In fact, Sugar should have come on this trip instead of her. She would have been Hank's second choice. And this whole clusterfuck would have been Sugar's cross to bear.

But then I'd have missed Hank's kiss, a small piece of her whispered.

It hadn't been that awesome. Sure, she hadn't had better, but not all men were good kissers.

Who was she kidding? That kiss had made the whole trip into space worth it. She wanted to touch her lips, where they still tingled from his amazing mouth. Most men were solid in the kissing department, but until now, she realized she hadn't even known how good it could be.

"Hello," Mima said, waving a hand before Lynette's face. "Are you in there?"

"Sorry, we've got a lot of pieces in motion right now." Lynette tried not to be annoyed. Usually she was great at giving contestants her full attention. She needed to shove Hank Carson and his breathtaking kisses into a hole so deep, she didn't think of them again this trip.

"I was talking about Terry," Mima prompted, sounding put out at Lynette's lack of response.

Sugar had not put this controversy to bed before sending the contestants into space. These issues should have been old news.

Having been voted out, Terry was no longer relevant. "Well, it doesn't matter, Mima, because we're here now and you don't have to see Terry ever again."

"I'll have to see her at the reunion episode," Mima said huffily.

"True." Lynette realized her lack of sleep was making her less than patient, because she wanted to say something else, something mean. Recognizing that she was about to lose her cool, she stashed Mima into the first suite she came to, instead of the one they'd assigned her, just to shut the woman up.

"The minute I see her, I want to slap her. Gouge her eyes out."

"I understand completely," Lynette said, pulling the door shut with Mima blessedly standing on the other side. "I'll come get you in one hour."

Mima caught the door before it shut. "I won't ever get over what she said to me."

"I'm sure." Lynette pried the other woman's fingers off the edge, enjoying the satisfying thunk of the door shutting.

"It's been days of that," Emma said, tossing her blonde hair back off her shoulder. Emma had those well-bred, girl-next-door classic good looks that were highlighted by an expert use of makeup and a perfect figure.

"Shoot me in the head and end it," Kyla agreed, also over Mima's drama. Her flawless olive skin and black hair were a frame for a lush mouth that was her best feature. Right now, it was held in a frown.

The three had been getting along when Lynette left, but this late in the game, it wasn't unusual for the contestants to start breaking down.

"Sounds tough," Lynette said, faking sympathy. She needed to get frosty. Things weren't going to get away from her because she was distracted. "You've got an hour before filming starts, so redo makeup and freshen up. This is going to be a crazy filming schedule. You are required to stay in your suites until I come get you."

Kyla went into her original assignment, but since Mima was in Emma's suite, Lynette put Emma in hers. She'd have to sort things out later, run up here and change things after the first cocktail.

She hustled to the shuttle to unleash the bachelor, spending the journey back through the circus and up to the third floor thinking about the kiss she and Hank had shared again, despite promising she wouldn't. It was dumb, but she felt all fluttery inside. And if they hadn't been interrupted, she might have climbed him like a tree.

Okay so she'd enjoyed it. That was fine. She was, after all, only human and Hank Carson was an amazing specimen. But she must, must, MUST not let it happen again. Now that the contestants were here, she had to be on her toes. They would film for the next three days, board the shuttle, and return to Earth. Then she had to get through the reunion show and the after party. After that, she could leave Hank's orbit for the rest of her life. Because nothing good ever came out of sleeping with your boss. And while the general public didn't know Hank's name, everyone she'd ever work for again not only knew him, but would judge her as an idiot if she slept with him. And she'd never work on a TV show again, not even one that centered around cleaning out hoarder houses.

After that stern talking to, she felt better. More in control. More centered.

As she returned to the landing area, the lights went out.

CHAPTER FOUR

*H*ank and Russ had been scrambling to get the video fully up and running as they followed Lynette's movement through the halls with the three contestants. Things weren't quite working the way they should be, but they were able to get the shots they needed. While Lynette went back to get the bachelor, they'd been watching Mima talking to herself in her room when everything went dark.

For a moment Hank was trapped in complete blackness, his only company Russ' heavy breathing.

With a loud pop, the green running lights placed at intervals along the floor came on.

"We'll miss the shot," Russ snarled. He grabbed a handheld video camera and ran out the door.

For a moment, Hank struggled to understand this latest twist, but then it hit him that Milton had been incorrect when he said losing power wouldn't happen again. Hank counted to ten rather than Hulk-out on Milton. He'd been willing to give the station owner the benefit of the doubt that everything with the power had been a temporary glitch. He had a firm policy of always starting out as the nice guy, letting the natives do their jobs. But even he had limits.

Unable to control his temper, he stomped to the circus, down one flight, into the banned south wing to the control room.

"You have to get it back on quickly," Milton said, so upset, Hank could hear him from the hall.

Hank slowed, figuring if Milton was dumb enough to leave the door open, it was okay to eavesdrop on their conversation.

Someone answered him but it was a mumble, so he crept closer.

"Carson will be furious if we can't get power back."

Damn right I'm furious.

"I told you a month ago we were on borrowed time with this," came the answer, and Hank realized it was the maintenance guy from his deep melodious voice.

Jackson seriously got under Hank's skin. He needed to let that go and concentrate on the latest calamity, but hearing his voice grated like nails on a chalkboard.

"Just get the lights on. I don't care how you do it," Milton said, his voice full of panic.

Hank peeked into the room to see Milton waving his arms, his face red, his chest heaving.

"I'm not a miracle worker. I have been warning you—"

"You know how to get them on. I know you do." Milton's voice calmed, as if something occurred to him. "If Carson doesn't pay us, I won't be the only person screwed. You have just as much invested in this as I do. That middle eastern prince isn't going to buy this place if we don't have the publicity we promised him. This is not the time to go soft on me."

"There is a way." Jackson held up his hand. "But I don't recommend it." His voice was intense but his pose was anything but. He lounged against the metal box, as if casual was his only mode. He needed a robe and a chalice and he'd be all set.

"Whatever has to be done, do it. It's do or die for us. They can't film without power and they won't pay us if they don't film."

That was for sure, Hank agreed silently. But he didn't like the sound of whatever the maintenance guy was proposing.

"If you're sure," Jackson said ducking back down behind the metal box.

"I'm sure."

"Okay then," came the muffled reply.

Hank leaned against the hall wall, debating his next move. He wasn't someone who backed down—ever—but he'd always thought he would cut and run if he ever felt he had to. Just because he'd never done it, didn't mean he couldn't.

Should he run now? Pull everyone out? Load them onto the shuttle that was still docked here and simply go home?

He didn't want to. He'd sunk a bunch of cash into this trip and he could tell by the way Milton spoke about money that Hank wasn't going to get a refund for his down payment from the old guy, that was for sure. But what he'd already paid was a sunk cost and he knew he shouldn't take that into account going forward. It was hard not to. Money to leave Earth wouldn't come again if he blew this chance. None of his backers would invest in him for another project if he packed up and returned home.

This place had been cobbled together with baling wire and a piece of chewing gum. Hank knew that now. He should have smelled a rat when Milton offered it at such a good price. This station had been a fraction of the cost of the Mars accommodations.

Hank went to find Lynette. He'd grab her and Russ and hear their thoughts. Although he was pretty sure he knew what Lynette would say.

The lights came on, cutting short his internal debate. It had happened so fast, Hank knew whatever had been done wasn't as big of a deal as Jackson had made it. Nothing bad could happen that quickly.

Maybe all wasn't lost after all. Relief spread through him. With the power on, he could make anything work.

Milton came around the corner. "Hank!" he exclaimed, clearly unnerved to see Hank in the hall. He took Hank's arm, hauling him back toward the circus. "I know I promised the lights wouldn't go out again—"

"You did," Hank interrupted, pissed that this shoot was ramping up to be a disaster. He might be staying, but that didn't mean he was happy about the conditions.

"But as you can see, we have it all well in hand." Milton talked over him. "Are you filming now?"

"We were trying to, but that's a bit hard in the dark." He pulled his arm away from the other man's grasp. "With no power."

"Great, great," Milton said gaily, as if Hank wasn't complaining.

"When I walked up, it sounded like—"

"Everything is perfect now, absolutely no problem at all. We have the power situation sorted and aren't going to have any more issues. That was a temporary blip."

"It didn't sound like it was temporary to me."

"It was bad, I'll give you that, but we're up and running now. You need to go back to what you were doing before the outage."

"I hope for all our sakes this is the last time we lose power." Hank tried to put a threat into the words, but it seemed to slide off Milton like butter on Teflon.

"I'll leave you alone so you can get things done." Milton ducked into a room that was marked Employees Only, shutting the door quickly behind him.

"Milton." Hank knocked on the door, not finished venting his frustration.

The lock clicked loudly, the sound final.

Hank banged another two times. "The lights better stay on, Milton! I mean it."

———

Lynette continued to the landing hangar, happy the lights had come back on much faster this time. Another loss of power wasn't a good sign, but at least they weren't going to be trapped in darkness forever. Her luck couldn't be that bad.

Could it?

No, it couldn't. She refused to believe it.

This season had been a breeze during the first two months of filming. So, of course it had to fall apart sometime. That was just what happened. Things went sideways and she pulled them back into line. That's what she did.

And the lights had come back on. So, she'd been right not to panic, even though a small part of her had wanted to run in circles screaming. She hated the dark. Had ever since she was a child back in North Carolina where she grew up feeling like a round peg in a square hole. It was only after she moved to LA that she finally found a place to fit in and a job she could focus all her energy on. It had been like coming home.

When she entered the landing bay, she found the bachelor, Max Botta, strolling out of the ship.

"You were supposed to wait for me to come for you," she said, feeling grumpy that multiple things were sliding off track. If Max wasn't following the rules, she would bet the contestants weren't either. Part of her wanted to turn right back around and race to the suites to make sure everyone was where they were supposed to be. But she couldn't leave Max wandering around the halls either. Decisions, decisions.

"The power went out on the ship," Max said, with that trustworthy earnestness that made women adore him. He was six feet tall and neither skinny nor fat, but that perfect lean muscle that made females (and some males) stop what they were doing and track him as he walked across a room. He had black hair and olive skin from the Italian heritage he'd been blessed with, and a mouth full of straight, white teeth that he flashed at her now in a companionable grin.

"When did the lights go out?" More power outages didn't sound like a good thing. The shuttle should have its own power source.

"A moment ago. It took me a while to find the exit."

She sighed. This place reminded her of a bad dystopian movie where the heroes had to get the biosphere back up and running or die. Next they'd end up with no food or water.

"Okay," she said, moving on, because he wasn't expected to stand there in the dark, although a piece of her would have preferred it if he had. For a second, she pondered why the shuttle had lost power, too, but then Max touched her arm, which was a no-no in her book. No one got to touch her. She gently moved her arm away, setting the boundary without being aggressive about it, since she still had a crucial week plus to work with him.

"Lynette," he said, in a tone that would have made some women's toes curl. "You look fantastic as always."

"Uh huh," she said, not buying it. She looked like crap and she knew it. She'd only had time to throw her hair in a messy ponytail and slap on some lip balm. She'd added a belt at the last minute so she wouldn't have to constantly pull her jeans up since they were stretched out from wearing them too long.

"Follow me and we'll get you squared away in your room," she said, redirecting them to the business at hand.

He followed her, thankfully not trying to butter her up again.

She knew his behavior was nothing personal. There was a certain type of man who simply enjoyed flirting with women. It was their go-to state, how they related with females. Lynette had always thought it was a dangerous way to behave. It signaled to other women that he was open to possibilities, even if he was currently in a relationship, which made it so that (in Lynette's opinion) he was more likely to always be cultivating a backup plan.

She didn't want a man who lived with backup plans as his steady state. That way led to easy outs. She wanted someone who was in it for the long haul, willing to fight through problems even if they weren't simple to solve. A partner should want to work at what needed to be worked at, and not trail a string of other possibilities behind him.

But that was her own personal strategy in choosing a man. Working on these shows, she'd had a lot of time to think through her preferences. She'd actually written a list at one after party when she and Sugar were drunk. First and foremost, she wanted a guy who wasn't too good looking, who didn't draw women's eyes to him at every turn. There was no reason to set herself up for a lifetime of beating other women off her man with a stick.

Not that she was an expert in love by any stretch. It had been years since she dated anyone, mainly because when she was shooting, she had zero time for anything else. And who wanted a girlfriend who dropped off the face of the earth (literally, sometimes) for months at a time? It would take a special kind of guy to be able to handle that kind of on-again, off-again relationship and still follow her rule that they had to be exclusive even when she was gone.

Max increased his pace to walk beside her. "Wow," he said, looking down into the circus, his voice excited for the first time. "This place is awesome."

She hoped the audience thought so, too. "We'll have the cocktails down there in less than an hour."

"Hello," Alphie yelled in his sing-song voice, catching them looking down at him.

"Who's that?" Max asked.

"No one," she answered, which was true. She increased her pace to leave the robot behind. "I'm afraid you were given a tiny room since you'll only be in it for a short amount of time," she said to distract Max, heading down a corridor which housed the command center, the hot tub, the kitchen, and Max's room.

"Of course," Max said, his voice full of fatalistic patience.

She had the feeling he'd expected to be treated a bit better than this, but he had a whole TV show whose only purpose was for him to find love and be adored and fought over by a passel of women. With all that, his attitude annoyed her.

Still, out of all the bachelors she'd worked with, Max was one of the better ones. He was consistently easygoing and wasn't into drama, on or off camera. And when Terry had badmouthed the other women to him, he'd promptly gotten rid of her, signaling to the rest of the contestants that he didn't want to hear about their infighting. Lynette had thought that was a smart move. Because the worst thing a bachelor could do was get embroiled in the petty squabbles of the contestants. They'd had shows where that had happened, and they'd been constantly dealing with chaos.

"Huh," Max said, looking at the bare, stripped down room with a single bed. "This is like an ancient monk's cell."

Lynette ignored the whining. "You have an hour and a half until you join the women for a cocktail at the bar. They will have time to socialize without you. The bathroom is through there and your clothes are here." She pointed to the tuxes and a box of his items. Men never seemed to struggle with wearing what had been decided for them, so she'd given him all his outfits at once.

He took it all in. "Do I get to choose the order of my dates or do you?"

Lynette braced for his pushback. "Hank has decided to have you pick their names from the grab bag."

"That's mildly annoying," he said with a frown. "I would prefer to choose."

"I know, but we can't have you telegraphing who is your favorite to the audience." At this point in the game, she always had to come clean to the bachelor that this was a TV show. "We're here for you to fall in love, but we're also here to give those at home the experience as well." She smiled at him. "Plus, you'll be glad you didn't have to choose, since it will cut down on the women complaining to you."

He opened his mouth to argue with her.

"You don't want to hurt their feelings, do you?"

"Well, no, but—"

"Then trust me when I tell you this is the way to keep the peace." Instead of staying to hear more arguments, she closed the door on his disappointment.

Inside her head, an internal warning went off telling her things were going wrong somewhere else. Lynette might ignore these warnings in her personal life, but she never, ever ignored them on set. Since there was only one place the drama could be brewing, she hustled to the women's rooms one floor down.

Female raised voices echoed along the hall, but she couldn't understand the words. She broke into a slow jog, the only type of running she participated in.

"That dress is mine!" someone screamed.

Lynette rounded the corner to see Russ' back, where he stood filming in the hallway.

"It was in my room," Mima said in a sing song voice.

"You know that dress was assigned to me," the usually sweet Emma snarled, as Lynette shimmied sideways past Russ, who stood like an immovable object to get the shot.

"It looks better on me," Mima said, her voice full of that awful mean-girl cadence heard in middle school.

Finally popping out on the other side of Russ, Lynette had to admit the dress did look great on Mima. But that was not the point. The point was that Lynette, in her haste to put Mima into a room, any room, she'd stashed her with Emma's suitcases. Crap.

It had been a beginner's blunder, something Lynette hadn't done since the early days of her career. "Okay, okay," Lynette said, raising her hands. "Let's settle down."

"Total clusterfuck," Kyla said with a laugh.

Lynette didn't need advice from the peanut gallery. "You," she said, pointing at Kyla. "Back in your room."

Kyla huffed, but trotted into her room dutifully. Lynette had suspected she wanted on the after-show, *Paradise*, more than she wanted Max Botta, and pissing Lynette off was the way to lose her chance, so she always followed direct orders.

One problem down. She turned to Mima. "This is my fault. I assigned you Emma's room by mistake."

From behind the closed door came more laughter. Lynette had to stop her sudden desire to take her frustration out on Kyla. As much as she wished it wasn't, the fault was her own. "Go take off that dress, Mima, and we'll switch rooms so everyone is with their own things."

Mima shifted her stance into one of total confrontation, arms crossed, head cocked to one side. "No way am I leaving this room. I like it. And I'm not bringing anything out to her. She wants her stuff, she can come get it."

Lynette felt a snap and knew it was her patience breaking. A cold, quiet wrath built inside her that she hadn't felt in the last three seasons.

"Uh oh," Russ whispered with relish.

She stepped into the other woman's space. "I did not ask you. That was an order. Get that dress off and return here so we can exchange rooms." She did not add the consequences. Mima knew exactly what was at stake. She might want Max more than *Paradise*, but like everyone who didn't win, *Paradise* was a nice consolation prize.

Mima debated her next move, her eyes narrowing.

Bring it, Lynette almost snarled, but stopped just in time. Blooper reel, blooper reel, blooper reel. She could not forget. Highlights from past seasons were often incorporated and she didn't want to end up on the mega hits list a second time. The first time, she'd fallen into the pool during a cocktail, reflexively grabbing two contestants and hauling them into the water with her. That had always been a crew favorite, much to her deep embarrassment.

From behind Kyla's door came more laughter.

Lynette ignored it with effort. "You've got one minute to comply." Lynette wasn't someone who liked confrontation, but she'd long ago learned that avoiding it in this situation would come back to bite her tenfold.

She and Mima had a stare-down.

Mima blinked. "Fine." She stomped inside her suite and tried to slam the door, but the portal was on some sort of soft close, so the effort was wasted.

The word bitch floated out to the hallway, but Lynette had not become one of the best in the business by having thin skin. Words didn't ever have to hurt her unless she let them.

Two down, one to go. "Emma, get whatever you brought in earlier and come back here."

Emma, who had always leaned toward mousy, did as directed without complaining that she wasn't going to wear a dress that Mima had had on her body, which is what Lynette half expected her to say.

"Thanks for the help," she snarled to Russ, and knew he was doing a closeup of her face. She considered decking him, but her rational brain reminded her she couldn't afford to have him out of commission. Instead, she turned her back, effectively shutting down his optics.

"Mean," he murmured.

She shot him the bird. Let him put that in the blooper reel.

Mima stomped out of the suite in her original clothes and the two women walked past each other, their eyes shooting hate lasers.

Their doors closed, and Lynette took a deep, centering breath. Okay that had sucked and was a mistake on her part, but they'd worked through it. This was going to be fine. Just a bump in the road.

Emma raced back in the hall. "That bitch destroyed all my things!" she wailed.

For a moment, Lynette's brain did nothing. She stood stock still.

Then her mind functioning returned.

Of course she had ruined Emma's things. Lynette wanted to scream, but instead stalked into the suite annoyingly followed by Russ still filming.

Mima had managed to toss all Emma's belongings into the floor and it looked like a clothing bomb had exploded.

But on closer inspection, she hadn't destroyed anything, probably because she hadn't had time to do real damage.

Lynette sighed. "Help me pick it all up, Emma."

They gathered all the clothes and put them on the small bed.

Lynette firmly put the blame on exactly who deserved it—her.

She should have paid attention to where she'd put the contestants. Now she'd orchestrated a war between the two women, and both of them would be pissed at Kyla for being so amused. No one liked to be laughed at. Which meant that tonight's cocktail would be a disaster.

"She ruined my dress!" Emma held it up and showed where the zipper had ripped.

"I'll get you another." Lynette took the dress, wishing Sugar were here so she could sew the zipper back in. Her skills were so much better than Lynette's, which were only marginal at best. "Get your makeup on and I'll be right back."

"Wait," said Russ from behind the camera. "Emma hold the dress and look down at it all sad."

All her anger wanted to shift to Russ for coming up with such a stupid idea. But instead of sharing her feelings, she handed the dress over to Emma for the shot. They were making TV here. She would not kill Russ for doing his job.

She would not.

Emma stared at the ripped zipper dolefully, one tear tracking down her beautiful cheek. Lynette was sure she wasn't faking it.

"Enough," Lynette said, gently taking the dress back, when she wanted to rip it out of Emma's hands. "I'll return with a new dress in a few."

"This wasn't my fault!" Emma said between sniffles.

"I know it wasn't. Go get your makeup on. Just remember we're heading toward the end, so things are going to get stressful." They'd warned the women in pre-filming training.

Emma nodded and dashed the tears with her hands.

Lynette ignored Russ as he followed her, double timing it to the command center, where she found Hank at the bank of computers.

One look at Hank and she knew she wasn't the only person having a bad day.

"The maintenance guy says we can't use all the cameras at once. We have to rotate them," Hank snarled.

"What?" Russ said, finally dropping the camera by his side.

"Ha!" Lynette said pettishly. "Sucks to have everything go sideways, doesn't it?"

Russ growled at her.

"What happened?" Hank asked, giving them his full focus.

"Lynette has her panties in a twist because the girls were fighting." Russ put his handheld camera on the desk. "I got it all on tape." Satisfaction filled his words.

Hank shook his head in puzzlement. "They're supposed to fight, especially at this stage."

"I made a mistake," she admitted.

"You don't make mistakes."

His loyalty touched her. "I did today." She dropped onto Hank's bed with a frustrated sigh. "I put Mima in Emma's room and she wrecked it for fun."

"I don't know how I'm expected to get the right shots if I don't have full access to all the cameras," Russ whined.

"How did that happen?" Hank asked unhelpfully, ignoring Russ.

She tried not to shift her anger to Hank as well. "Did I not just say I fucked up?"

Hank patted the air in an annoying gesture she assumed was supposed to calm her. Instead, she had to grind her teeth to keep from snapping his fingers off. She needed to get out of here. Stat. Go someplace and calm down.

"I need to bring Emma a new dress." She rose, crossing to the clothing racks. She'd long ago made a rule that only one party dress was handed out at a time. Hanging the ripped dress on the rack, she grabbed Emma's next dress, wondering how she would sew the zipper back into the old one, since they had no clothes to spare.

CHAPTER FIVE

*T*he first cocktail party in space was in full swing. They'd spent most of the first hour filming the women walking down the stairs. Hank had them redo it several times because their hearts hadn't been in it. They should have been full of grace and elegance and excitement. Emma especially had been like a pissed-off gazelle, stomping down the Metal stairs with loud clangs at each footfall.

As much as he'd tried to convince her otherwise, Lynette had been right. The earlier squabble had the three women furious at each other. He was going to need to bring the bachelor in early to shake the ladies out of their cutting remarks and side-eye snarls.

Last night while he laid there trying to sleep, he'd gone back and forth in his mind about how to run the next three dates. Did he let the bachelor choose? The audience would be enthralled by that, but it might tip Max's hand and cut the tension of the last rose ceremony, something that wasn't good for final night ratings. Hank had finally decided to have a simple grab-bag. That would hide which way Max was leaning and keep the girls from more infighting if they weren't chosen for the coveted first date.

Max Botta didn't disappoint when he came down the stairs. He looked like an ad for a sports car come to life. Everyone except Russ, who was holding a camera, clapped and Max flashed his unforgettable smile. Standing nearby, Emma let out a heartfelt sigh, just as Hank hoped every woman watching would exhale with longing.

Max gave cheek kisses to each of the woman down the line they'd formed, got a whiskey in a highball from an excited Alphie, then came back to mingle. "How are you ladies doing now that we've gotten into space?"

"Good," Kyla purred, her voice the proper mix of excitement and sexy she'd most likely practiced.

"Could I steal you for a moment, Max," Mima said, curling her arm through his.

The other two women started as if they'd been shocked by a live wire. Mima had beaten everyone else to the punch by circumventing the opening chit chat.

She pulling him to a window, where they could have a small amount of privacy examining the stars.

"That bitch," Kyla snarled.

"She's always so greedy," Emma said with uncharacteristic snark.

"He didn't even get to take a sip of his drink," Kyla agreed.

Hank wasn't pleased with the tenor of their conversation, but they could edit some of it out. Audiences didn't like it when things got too nasty. Still, he could work with the film. Massage it. He had a deft hand when it came to telling a story the audience loved.

Both women stood silent, looking grim and ready for battle. Kyla waited two minutes before going to break in. "Can I steal you for a moment?" she asked, knowing full well that the standard time with the bachelor should have been ten minutes.

Max, for his part, had been trained to always go when asked, but he gave Mima a disappointed hug as he crossed with Kyla to two chairs side by side, facing another viewport.

"You going to count this down?" Lynette asked, showing up beside where Hank had stationed himself next to Alphie at the bar. The countdown put the contestants on notice that they were going to have to gather in a set amount of time.

Lynette must feel like things were deteriorating too rapidly, but Hank wasn't so sure. "Not quite yet."

"Would you like a drink?" Alphie asked her, his happy painted-on smile joining the peppy voice.

Lynette made a face at him. "Go away." Her meanness, even to a robot, showed she was on the edge.

Hank found that very worrying. "Are you okay?" he asked, shifting his attention away from where it should have been to his right hand.

"Of course."

Looking closer at her pinched mouth and tapping foot, he wasn't sure that was true. Was this still about placing people in the wrong rooms? "One mistake isn't a big deal."

"I don't make those kinds of mistakes," she said, crossing her arms.

"I know you don't. You're the best in the business." Hank needed to get her back on track. He wasn't used to having to talk Lynette of all people off the ledge. "Put it aside. You are human. Mistakes will happen once in a blue moon."

"A drink will help you put aside your troubles!" Alphie added.

Lynette turned her back to the bar to block out the robot. "I feel like all of this is sliding out of control. The contestants fighting this badly when they'd been fine with each other before is only a piece of it. The power outages are giving me feelings of impending doom."

Hank hesitated a moment before touching her hand. They both jumped at the electricity in the contact. He dropped his arm to his side and rubbed away the feeling on his tuxedo pants.

Her gaze met his, her eyes doleful. "This thing between us is also a large mistake."

It hurt to hear her call him a mistake, but he knew it wasn't professional to mix business with pleasure. Part of him was tempted to kiss her again, to prove she was wrong. Without meaning to, he leaned down into her airspace, his gaze fixed on her lips, wondering if that first kiss had simply been some sort of aberration. Maybe he only had to kiss her again to realize the first time had been a fluke.

Her eyes widened and a look of panic crept in, making him straighten. He'd never had a woman recoil from him, but her stiffened shoulders made him wonder if he was about to have the experience.

Although maybe she was right. Yes, he wanted her, which surprised him, but he could control himself. Wait until this trip from hell was over. After filming wrapped, he would invite her out for a drink, he decided. See if there was anything there. But for now, he would place it firmly away from his uppermost mind and concentrate on the large accumulating problems surrounding them.

"Don't worry!" Alphie crooned in sympathy, leaning between them. "I have the power outages under control. I've taken over the situation."

"What?" Hank and Lynette said together.

"Back off, Mima," Kyla screamed from across the room, tearing away their focus.

Hank had been about to kiss her and she had been about to let him. Again. This rejoicing at his nearness had to stop.

What was wrong with her? She'd lost all her common sense. She'd always thought women acting like fools when they were in love was not only a terrible cliché, but also a sign they were idiots. She would never behave like that. Obviously, she had been wrong about the basics of her own character.

This show was going to be the end of her career. She dropped her head in her hands to try to block out how great Hank looked in his tux, so she could focus on giving herself a strong scolding.

"You don't give me orders," Mima snarled.

Lynette looked up to see Mima crowding Kyla off the sofa by smushing next to Max.

Kyla slapped at her. "Bitch, you've already had your turn with him."

The physical altercation was a violation of rule number one. Normally she would race across the room and haul them all apart. Instead, she leaned back on the bar and said, "Well, shit." Her mismanagement had led to this.

It became crystal clear to her that when Hank Carson had kissed her, he had sucked out her brains, like some sort of alien in a horror movie.

At Kyla's shove, Mima toppled into the floor, grabbing Kyla's hair as she fell, taking Kyla with her in the process.

The red rose of Mima's dress swirled with the sapphire blue of Kyla's as they rolled across the floor, girl slapping at each other and screaming.

Max still sat, pressed back into the sofa, horror on his face.

Well, what had he thought would happen? He was on a show where women vied to marry him in a modern-day gladiator fight. He had to realize blood might be shed.

A vase with two dozen silk red roses supported by clear marbles crashed to the ground, the balls bouncing in all directions, sounding like scattershot in a war.

The noise seemed to jerk Hank out of his shocked tableau. "Ladies, ladies!" Hank launched himself across the room.

While the show loved (and even encouraged) the occasional verbal fight, the rules stated that no one was allowed to physically abuse another contestant. That meant someone could, and would, intervene. Rarely were these scenes shown on TV, because they tried to keep the staff out of view at all costs. Showing the support staff broke the illusion that all this happened without interference.

Alphie leaned across the bar to peer at her with his huge eyes. "I've made you a Rockin' Cosmos." He tenderly sat a martini class filled with something blue, a piece of orange peel floating in the bottom. It looked awful. "It's my specialty," he said in his cheery tone. "It cures all ills."

"This is a mess," she informed him, picking up the drink to peer inside. She dearly needed something. Anything. Even this electric blue concoction which probably tasted awful.

"Try it. No one has ever been disappointed," he encouraged in a sing-song. "It will pep you right up."

Willing to do anything to stop her internal struggle, she took a cautious sip. It tasted like it looked. Blue with a hint of orange, if blue had a flavor. Kind of sweet with a hint of melancholy. It suited her mood perfectly. "Good," she agreed, watching as Hank caught Mima under the arms and hauled her backwards, Russ right in the middle filming.

"Calm down," Hank ordered, trying and succeeding in catching his balance as he slid on marbles. Instead of looking awkward, he appeared dashing and handsome. Of course. If she had gone over there, she would have landed in a heap on her ass.

"I knew you'd like it," Alphie said, his voice filled with fake pleasure.

"That bitch is hogging Max," Mima screamed.

"This is all my fault," she explained to the robot, taking a long swallow.

"I doubt that, Ms. Smith," he said, his voice now filled with sympathy. "Humans are responsible for their own behavior."

"I messed up," she confessed. This is why you couldn't trust robots. They so easily weaseled their way into your confidence.

"Ladies, please," Max said weakly, looking disappointed and tired rather than excited by the squabble.

"If anyone is a hog, it's you," Kyla said, trying to get her hair back into its high pony, but her extensions had come loose on one side, turning her from glamorous to bedraggled.

How quickly someone can lose that polished shine. Lynette took another sip to reflect upon this new observation.

"You both know nothing physical is allowed." Hank looked around and found her. His face changed from stern to worried at whatever he saw.

She realized she was doing her rendition of a woman at the end of her rope and tried to look competent, instead of morose.

This was her purview. In fact, he shouldn't even be over there. She handled these kinds of things. They'd only been filming for a few hours. She should be on top of everything, but instead lethargy nipped her. It was the kiss. It had stolen her will to rule with an iron fist. She had trouble caring about anything else, least of all two women fighting over sitting next to Max Botta.

This is why she had to stuff her once hidden feelings for Hank back into the vault. Nothing good would come of this. She had to remain strong.

Not knowing what else to do, she toasted him.

"Lynette," he said calmly.

She raised an eyebrow.

"Could you join me, please?" he asked, his voice carefully controlled.

She sighed, took a last gulp of her drink and hopped off her stool. "Rule number one states what, Kyla?" she asked on her way over, already sad to leave her drink behind. It had been a perfect addition to her blue mood.

"No physical fighting. But this wasn't my fault! That bitch started it." Kyla dramatically pointed to Mima.

"You're the bitch," Mima snarled where she still hung from Hank's hands. The slit in her dress had ripped upwards and now began above her hip.

"We were going to do a grab bag for who gets to go on the first date with Max, but I think with this drama, we'll let Emma go first," Lynette declared, not bothering to run it past Hank. No one would get a benefit from this display.

"Yay, yay, yay," Emma squealed, jumping up and down, hopping in a circle. Her mousy tendencies had finally worked to her advantage.

Lynette felt genuine pleasure for her. She may not have a crazy in-your-face personality, but Emma was an intelligent, amazing woman. Going against one of her most trusted rules to never take sides, she found she was rooting for her.

Max smiled in relief and stood, the action not as smooth as usual since he slid on a couple marbles and had to do a shuffle step. "Shall we go to your suite?" he asked, cutting the night short.

"I would be honored," Emma cooed. She took hold of his arm and smiled up at him, so sweet, Lynette knew it would make perfect TV.

"I would be honored," Mima mimicked in a high voice.

"Zip it or I'll jettison you out the airlock," Lynette said mildly, not even sure if the station had an airlock, but it sounded good.

She found she was faking it, since most of her didn't seem to care that things had gotten out of control.

She watched Max and Emma walk up the spiral staircase with a detached air she'd never felt in her life, noting Russ trailing along behind them with a camera.

As a type A+ personality, she didn't do detached. In fact, she didn't believe in it. She wasn't sure what was in Alphie's drink, but she took back every mean thing she'd ever thought about him. That liquid was pure blue gold.

Hank stuck Mima onto a silver overstuffed chair and returned to Lynette's side, kicking marbles out of the way as he moved.

"You think that was wise?" he murmured.

"Can it make things worse?"

"You haven't made a mistake we can't recover from. I'm telling you, you're the best in the business. All of this can be edited out."

"Uh huh," she said, unconvinced. "I need to heat their dinner and set up the video connection." They would be streaming in a country crooner to serenade Max and Emma so they could dance for the camera. Then the couple would climb into the hot tub and make out. After, they would return to Emma's suite and things would fade to black. She just needed to hang in there long enough to get through it. After that, she could agonize over the fact that she wanted a man who was all wrong for her.

Hank gave her all his considerable attention. "Are you okay?"

"I'm not sure," she said honestly. "You need to get these two into the box to do post fight interviews." Sometimes what the women said about each other when they were still hot around the collar was worth TV ratings gold. Lynette's favorite was *I'm not here to make friends.*

"We need to talk," Hank said, grabbing her arm and pulling her to the stairs.

"Ooooh look who's in trouble now," Mima sing-songed.

Lynette was seriously over her, and turned back to tell her about it, but Hank marched her up the stairs instead.

As they came around the spiral, he pointed a finger at them. "You two better be sitting right there when I get back."

"Yeah, yeah." Mima rearranged her body on the chair with a flounce.

They went around another spiral. "I mean it Mima. Don't make me disqualify you."

Kyla laughed. "That would be awesome."

"Shut up bitch," Mima snarled.

"You shut up."

"Too bad you can't do anything but copy me, you're such an idiot."

"Nice dress, dumb ass," Kyla said with another annoying laugh.

Lynette sighed as Hank pulled her into an unused room. "Their relationship is toast," she said vaguely, still feeling the wondrous zone of nothingness.

"Did you take something?"

"Alphie gave me his special."

"What?" Hank peered closely at her eyes.

"A Rockin' Cosmos. Best thing I've ever had." She needed to get the recipe before she left.

Hank shook her, which Lynette found unpleasant. "Stop that," she ordered swatting at his hands, not liking that he was ruining the best feeling she'd had today.

"I need you frosty. You need to get your head in the game."

She found she hated the game. "I fucked up by putting them in the wrong rooms and started World War Three," she explained to him slowly.

"So what? This shit happens every season. Shake it off."

Easy for him to say.

She felt unreasonably annoyed with him. "If you didn't keep hauling us to the middle of nowhere to film, we wouldn't end up in these situations," she pointed out, warming up to be pissed, instead of sad. That was so much better.

"We're up here because we're the best. We take situations that other shows couldn't dream of and make them happen." Pride rung in his words.

She'd spent most of her adult career being buoyed by his pep talks. She wasn't feeling it right now. In fact, she was over all of this. She was especially over him. "This trip was stupid, Hank. I knew it and yet here I am." She threw out her arms in a dramatic gesture to the damaged wiring hanging from the ceiling.

"If it was so 'stupid,' why are you even here?" he asked in a snarl.

"You want to know why I made this colossal mistake?"

"Yeah, I do. I really do."

She gave a slow twirl, like a game show hostess displaying the beaten walls and sad metal furniture. "Why I lost my common sense and came here?"

He folded his arms across his broad, hot, manly chest, the black suit jacket pulling tight to show off his body. "Please tell me why you were so stupid."

She should stop, but the brakes on her mouth weren't working. "Because I had some dumb crush on you." She stalked to the door and tried to throw it open, but it was too heavy and she had to jam one tennis shoed foot to keep it from banging shut.

"You did?" he asked from behind her.

She would deck him if she wasn't a pacifist. "I'm going to get the date started," she snarled. And left yummy Hank Carson standing alone in the battered room.

CHAPTER SIX

*H*ank stood frozen staring at nothing as the door shut under its own weight.

Lynette had a crush on him. Wow. He'd felt her rejection earlier loud and clear. But she'd declared that she had liked him, maybe for a long time.

Past tense.

But still. He found he enjoyed the thought of her wanting him a little too much. For a moment, he allowed himself to play with the idea of rushing after her. Pulling her into his arms and kissing her again. The feel of her lips under his had been one of the best he'd had in a long time.

The women he'd dated had all been beautiful, but if he was honest, most of them had been as self-preoccupied as he'd been. They'd enjoyed dating him because they only saw the surface of him. He hadn't had anything deep and lasting in a long time. Maybe, if he was honest with himself, never. Lynette was a woman who would be deep and worthy, someone he could wake up to every day, someone he could rely on to have his back, who followed through on every promise.

He opened the door to go find her and stopped.

He had a show to produce, footage that needed his immediate attention or it would go stale. And she'd sounded like whatever flame she might have held for him was over. The idea he had something and lost it before he even realized it didn't sit well with him. He wanted to talk this out, explore what she'd meant when she said she had a crush. But this wasn't the time. Both their careers were on the line here.

Instead of following his heart, he went back down the spiral staircase. Mima and Kyla sat where he'd left them, the thought of missing out on *Paradise* keeping their asses glued to the chairs, although they were clearly still both pissed. "Interview time," he said.

They both groaned, agreeing with each other for the first time all day.

"Let's go," he said, not in the mood. But this is what he did. This was his passion.

They trouped to the interview room on the first floor. Leaving Mima out in the hall on the chair they'd put there for that reason, he went inside the filming room they'd set up with Kyla to interview her about the big fight.

"So," he said, after turning on the camera. "Tell me about how you're feeling about Max Botta."

"I'm coming to like him more every second I'm in his presence. I'm surprised at how deeply my feelings go."

He nodded, because he was surprised by his feelings, too. For once, he truly understood what a contestant was feeling.

Why couldn't she keep her damn mouth shut? It had been obvious that it had never even crossed Hank's mind that she could want him, even after their steamy kiss.

"Idiot," she whispered.

Breaking into a light jog, she made it to Emma's suite on the double to find Max confronting Russ.

"I'm asking you to keep the camera out of our faces," Max said, in the exaggerated slow voice of someone about to lose their cool.

Emma sat on her sofa with a stricken look on her face.

"The contract you signed says I can film any way I need to," Russ said in his annoying monotone, but in a louder volume, signaling that he, too, had his temper rising.

"Okay, let's take a deep breath here," she said in her reasonable voice. "Russ you stand three feet back at a minimum." She pulled Russ back more like four, but he didn't stop filming the couple. "How about I work on your surprise while you two talk?" She tried to put excitement in her tone, but it was hard in the shadow of her idiotic move seconds ago with Hank.

She almost suggested Emma and Max get into the hot tub, but then realized she'd never checked the temperature after they'd lost power. Sloppy, sloppy, sloppy. One more example she was losing her edge.

"Talk about what?" Max asked, becoming difficult for the first time.

That was okay. Every cast member went through their moment. She could and would manage with this. "How about your last relationship woes?"

"Done," he said, narrowing his eyes at her. "She had trouble with expressing her feelings."

Not a surprise. "What about the most embarrassing moments?"

"She got her eyelid stuck in a zipper."

"What?" Lynette was temporarily derailed by this. "How is that possible?" *Don't get sucked in! You have to check the hot tub temperature, set up the satellite feed and heat up dinner.*

"Well," Emma said, her face turning a pretty shade of pink.

"Never mind." She waved a hand, refocusing on Max. "Favorite color?"

"Hunter green," Max snarled.

"Pink," Emma corrected, looking mildly hurt.

"Whatever," Max said, clearly not caring.

Lynette kind of agreed with him. It didn't matter what someone's favorite color was after you got past the age of ten. Her own favorite color happened to be purple, which she never wore at work. She had to blend in, become part of the backdrop. Blacks and navy blue had become her uniform. "If you think you might marry this woman, surely you have something to talk about?" She should have more finesse but come on. This was one of his top three choices for forever. "How about having a drink?" She walked over to a hidden cabinet and opened it. It wasn't good to have more right after the drinks they had at the cocktail, but screw it. She'd found her earlier drink had helped significantly.

"Now you're talking," Max said, crossing over to pick up a highball glass and the whiskey bottle. "Emma?"

"Is there any wine?"

Having navigated the bump, Lynette slipped out to get the live feed set up.

Inside the command center, she saw on one monitor that Hank was interviewing Mima. Good. At least that was going as planned.

She pulled up the live feed they'd established yesterday, following Russ' instructions to the letter. An error popped up.

All outside communications blocked.

What did that mean?

She considered calling Russ back to look at it. He was still filming in Emma's suite, locked in total concentration and wouldn't be thrilled if she interfered again. So, instead she went in search of Milton.

She found him having a drink at the bar with Alphie.

"Lynette." His smile held forced jollity.

She didn't bother with a greeting. "Are the outside comms down?"

Milton nodded, looking wary. "I'm afraid so. We had to give some things up to get the power back on."

"Want another Rockin' Cosmos?" Alphie asked in his cheery voice.

"No." She focused in on Milton, noting the ashen color to his face. "Are you okay?"

"Yes, of course," he said, straightening from his slouch.

A bad thought occurred to her. "If we can't communicate with the outside world, doesn't that leave us in trouble if something goes wrong?"

Milton waved his hands to push aside her worries. "No, no, we can always divert power if we need to. But you need so much electricity for filming, it hogs up our reserves. I hadn't realized how many cameras you'd put in place."

She tried not to think of what could go wrong. It was her job to pre-plan for emergencies, but she realized she'd have to stop thinking the worst or she'd run screaming with fear.

"Is dinner on its way to suite 201?" she asked, trying to move on to the next issue.

"It certainly is," Alphie assured her. "I sent it by droid myself a few moments ago."

"Thanks, Alphie," she said, and took off at a fast trot back to the suite to settle them into dinner. Then she'd go to the command center to call up the footage they'd brought with them. Thank God they'd pre-taped the concert on Earth before they left just in case.

When she took off the metal covers, dinner didn't look great. The food had an odd sheen that she suspected meant it had been freeze dried at one point, but she managed to get them eating. "We've got a surprise in a moment," she said, injecting as much enthusiasm as possible in her voice.

"I love surprises," Emma cooed.

Lynette hated surprises. She hated that moment where she had to fake her excitement about something she didn't want at Christmas or her birthday. The best moments were those that were planned out to a T. "You'll love this one," she promised, pulling Russ into the corridor. "I need you to call up the canned version of Texas Pete."

"I thought we were streaming him live?"

"Milton says they had to shut down outside communications to conserve power so we can run the cameras."

"What?" Russ' usually expressionless face crunched in worry. "That means we can't call for help," he said, echoing her earlier thoughts.

"If the choice is filming or Texas Pete live, we have to film. That's what we're here for."

He gave a curt nod of agreement. "I'll get the tape running, then see what I can find out," Russ promised.

Lynette went to top their wine glasses with what appeared to be a nice chardonnay. She was tempted to pour herself a glass but discarded the idea when she remembered how loopy Alphie's Rockin' Cosmos made her. She wasn't a big drinker and this sudden desire for alcohol surprised her. And she'd been worried about Milton earlier. Maybe the two of them could start the space chapter of Alcoholics Anonymous.

Max and Emma chatted as they finished their dinner, Max at his most charming. He had thankfully refocused on Emma and they'd talked about their plans for the future. Emma was a cancer researcher who'd made huge strides in understanding how cancer spread in the body. She could move anywhere in the world that had a research university, including LA, which was where the rented mansion they'd live in after the show was located. If Max chose her.

At least the two were talking about the future. Max's career as a Formula One race car driver was on the wane, and he planned to go into sports casting. LA was a great town for that.

On the screen that took up the right-hand wall, Texas Pete popped into view. "Howdy y'all," he crooned, almost appearing to be live.

Emma squealed in excitement.

"I'm gonna sing you some songs. Here is the first one, written for lovers like you." Without a pause, Pete broke into song, so that it wasn't obvious he was canned. The camera panned out to show his band playing in the background. "You bring me joy like a spring day on a wheat field," Pete sang.

"Want to dance?" Max asked Emma and the smile she gave him made Lynette's heart hurt it was so full of happiness.

Would she ever smile that way at anyone? Sure, she had a thing for Hank, but if she smiled at him like that, he'd run screaming from her, instead of pulling her into his arms. Would she ever smile that way at someone and have them smile back at her?

The song ended and Max leaned slowly down for a kiss, his lips barely brushing hers.

It was so sweet, Lynette sighed and gave in to temptation, pouring a glass of wine in an unused water glass.

Pete went into another love ballad and the dancing began again.

Lynette slumped into the corner overstuffed chair, wallowing in self-pity.

She deserved a man who loved her back. She was worth more than some cheap crush on a man who hardly knew she existed. She was better than this, and certainly better than a tawdry fling. Being alone was better than being someone's secret booty call.

Suddenly she remembered she hadn't checked the hot tub. She popped to her feet and raced down the hall.

Hank was exhausted after finishing the two postmortems with Mima and Kyla. He sent Milton an intership communication and went to the command center, playing with the idea of getting a couple minutes of sleep.

He found Russ bent over the consoles, typing frantically.

"What's up?" he asked, almost not wanting to know. He looked longingly down at his single bed. The pillow appeared fluffy, perfect to cradle his aching head. Things had gone so wrong, he almost regretted his decision to film here.

"Milton has shut down the outside communications link so we can't stream the singers we have lined up."

"We knew things might be dicey on that front. That's why we brought the backup." He fumbled around in a box that should have aspirin in it. Somewhere. Please God let there be something to help his aching head.

"Yeah, but I'm starting to wonder what he's up to. I'm locked out of a bunch of areas I had access to before."

Digging to the bottom of the box, Hank's fingers hit a bottle that rattled promisingly. He hauled it up and popped off the top and took two dry. A bitter taste filled his mouth. "You'd better leave it alone. I'm starting to think this place can't handle the slightest pressure without falling apart."

"I think you're right," Russ agreed, still typing.

"The hot tub is cold," Lynette announced at the doorway. "I've turned it on, but it will take hours to heat back up. Dammit. Now what am I supposed to do with them?" She dropped onto his bed.

Hank was tempted to join her, but instead located a couple bottles of water and tapped her on the shoulder with one.

She glanced up and he handed her the water. "Thanks," she said, her voice so filled with gratitude, he leaned down to hug her.

He stopped just in time. He wasn't going to make the pressure between them worse than it already was. That would solve nothing.

Or would it?

Jackson, the maintenance man, took the moment of indecision away from him by striding into the room. "Who turned on the hot tub?" he growled in his melodious voice, managing somehow to sound pissed and sexy at the same time.

"I did." Lynette stood, her old take-no-shit persona clicking into place.

Hank found he liked that she wasn't melting in the face of the handsome maintenance man. The annoyance he'd felt when the man walked in receded a bit.

"No one can turn that on. We don't have the power to run it."

"How did you even know I'd done it?"

"The power drain set off an alarm I set up."

"Are you that worried about the power?" Hank didn't find this news reassuring. Milton promised that everything would be okay, but he was starting to see that Milton's promises weren't worth the paper they were printed on.

"Of course I'm worried. We're limping here. You should speed up your filming." Then he turned and left without another word, leaving them all in a shocked silence.

"If they're admitting it, it's bad," Russ pointed out.

He was right. Milton might lie, but this Jackson-the-Adonis had given them the straight scoop.

"I think we should take his word for it," Hank decided. "Let's speed up again."

"They have to sleep," Lynette pointed out. "The schedule was already super tight at four days."

"Can we cut it even more?"

She dipped her head back and forth. "Lower the 'days' to twenty hours each maybe?"

"Yeah." Hank shuffled the schedule in his mind. "We haul the other two down to the circus and let them play some sort of game to decide who gets the second night with Max as soon as we've gotten some sleep ourselves. That gives us all sleep but speeds up the cadence."

"You sure we have time to rest?" Lynette asked, but not aggressively. More like she hoped he'd talk her out of it.

"Yeah. Let's grab," he looked at his watch, "six hours and then wake Emma and Max for interviews with you while I do the game downstairs with Russ." He paused. "Anything else going wrong?"

"No," Lynette said.

"Not yet," Russ added.

"Then let's get some shuteye while we can."

CHAPTER SEVEN

*L*ynette left the command center feeling defeated. Not with the show. The show would be okay if they could get all their filming done before the whole place shut down. Besides, they could always get on the shuttle and go home early if things got too bad.

It was this thing she had for Hank that was making her sad.

Pushing into her bare room, she shed her clothes and ran the shower. She'd somehow ended up with the largest bathroom on the station, bigger even than the ones in the contestants' suites. She had to admit, she was happy to have a separate shower away from the toilet. Standing naked with her hand under the stream, she waited for the ice cold water to warm.

I'm being stupid. Snap out of it, woman. There are other men in the sea.

When she got home, she'd go out on some dates. Have a social life for once.

Feeling somewhat buoyed, she brushed her teeth. The water warmed and she stepped beneath it, giving her body a needed scrub. She lathered the shampoo, imagining she washed Hank right out of her hair.

She'd sleep in her clothes just in case more shit went wrong, she decided as she reluctantly turned off the water.

Throwing on a t-shirt and underwear, she brushed out her hair on autopilot. She should be exhausted but instead she contemplated the conundrum of her feelings for Hank. It had turned into her favorite internal topic.

No more working with him after this wrapped. That stopped now.

She'd apply to work on another show the minute her feet hit Earth. Because seeing him in a tux or in jeans or hell, in a clown suit, just made her want him more.

If she got a new job fast, this colossal cluster fuck of a shoot might not even be common knowledge. She could disappear onto another set. Poof! Gone. Like a ninja into the night.

A soft knock came at the door.

Sighing, she went to open it, gearing up for another emergency. Perhaps someone crying over a broken fingernail.

She opened it a crack, her brush still in her hand. Hank stood without his tux suit jacket in a white shirt, black pants, his black bow tie undone but still around his neck. "More problems?" she asked, not inviting him in.

He held up two bottles of beer. "I came with a peace offering." He gave her a heart-stopping half smile.

She ruthlessly crushed down the pitter patter of her heart. "Go away, Hank. I'm not in the mood."

"Let me in Lynette," he said so gently, so far from a demand, her walls began to crumble.

She tried to build them back up. "It's a bad idea." He was her kryptonite, the one thing that always brought her good sense to its knees. This was the person who always made her want to dig deep and give him 110%, the person she knew could take her heart and stomp it into oblivion. She needed to keep the door not only shut, but locked and barricaded.

"Yeah." He gave her a lopsided smile that was so reluctant, she knew he was resisting it as hard as she.

If he'd come on strong, she would have stayed strong too, to keep him out. She would have slammed the door in his arrogantly handsome face. But this Hank, this man who seemed exhausted and slightly defeated—she couldn't resist him.

Ignoring the piece of her mind that shouted this is a terrible idea, she let the lion through her door.

Immediately, he filled the space with his presence. Even a Hank slightly defeated was still a large force. With him came the spicy male scent with an underlying tang of cinnamon. Her stomach tingled and she turned to fluff her pillows and sit on her bed so he wouldn't see the desire on her face.

He twisted off the bottle top and handed a beer to her, making good on his promise. Then he opened his own and took a long pull.

"I don't really like beer," she said like an idiot, but what was she supposed to say to this man? She took a tentative sip.

"No?" He'd seen her drink plenty of beer. Every wrap party had kegs of it, the amber liquid overflowing red silo cups, spilled across the sticky floor, while dance music filled the room and lighting technicians and key grips whooped it up as they boogied down. She'd always stayed until the first person threw up. Then she left. It was a firm rule. That way she had plausible deniability when the bigwigs complained later.

"Seems to be the social thing to do." But she found this beer was tasting pretty good. Bitter, just like her current mood.

Hank took the only chair in the small room, but even sitting he had a hum of energy that attracted people to him like flies to honey. "Out of nowhere, we seem to have developed something weird between us."

She barked a half laugh in shock, not expecting a direct assault on the issue. "You think?" Weird was his word. Hers would be an attraction on a deep and visceral level. At least on her part.

He held up a hand to stop her from interrupting. "And there is really only one way I see to deal with it."

"You don't say?"

Next, he'd go into a long speech about how they weren't good for each other, about their mutual career risk, the show, filming, etc, etc, etc. She took a long drink of her beer to brace her nerves, ready to agree so she could get him the hell out of her room. She never should have let him in. She should never have laid her heart out before a pirate like Hank Carson. This was a man who had a never-ending, revolving set of women hanging off his arm, all gorgeous and so very tall.

"I figure we need to have sex, to get it out of our systems."

Beer went down the wrong pipe as she inhaled, spurring a coughing fit. "Wait, what?" Was he insane?

"We've worked together what? Six years?"

"Eight," she said, somewhat insulted he'd forgotten when she counted every one.

"Right. And we've never had anything like this happen to us. Don't you find it odd?"

She didn't, actually, because she'd had a crush on him for much longer than she cared to admit. Rather than answer, she coughed a few more times to fully clear her lungs.

"I figure it's all situational. We need to burn through it and it will all go away."

"Burn through it?" she asked, trying to think through the implications. Her first thought was not that it was a terrible idea, but rather that she could have this man, no strings attached. Just once. Would she risk embroiling herself deeper so that she could run her hands over his amazing body?

"Yeah. We have sex for the next," he looked at his watch, "five hours while everyone else sleeps. When we get up in the morning, things will have gone back to normal."

Five hours…

"You think?" she asked, impressed at how casual her voice sounded when inside, she was so revved up, her head was spinning.

He was insane. That was the only explanation. This had to be the dumbest idea she'd ever heard.

"You know how sometimes you need a cheeseburger? But if you don't get one, it just builds and builds until you end up eating four of them and you feel sick?"

"You think I'm a cheeseburger?" Wait, what?

He laughed. "No, not you, this thing between us." He pointed back and forth between them.

For the first time in her life, Lynette considered if she had it in her to have a one-night stand. With a man who she not only suspected she was in love with, but who thought of her as a cheeseburger. Could she have him and walk away?

Yes, she decided, ignoring the part of her brain that pointed out she'd just decided she was worth more than a one-night stand mere hours ago.

She'd never be able to work with him again. Ever. This would be it.

But since she'd already decided she wasn't ever working with him again, she saw no downside.

If they'd had anyone else from the crew with them but Russ, they would already have been outed with the weird vibes between them. Thankfully, Russ was so oblivious, he hadn't noticed. And he wouldn't notice anything had changed if she could play it cool.

The question was, could she have him and not end up ruining sex with any other man in the future?

Or maybe a better question was if she walked away, would she always regret saying no?

She thought she would regret walking more than she'd regret not doing the wise thing. At least with his proposal, she wouldn't be tempted to assume they might stay together and make a fool of herself. Besides, maybe he would suck in bed. "Okay," she said, but even to her own ears, it sounded doubtful.

⌣

This is a terrible idea.

He couldn't wait.

Hank forced himself to put his beer on the floor, the action casual, when he wanted to jump onto the bed and roll her onto her back. "I'm caught up on all my shots. You?" The last thing they needed was a pregnancy from a one-night stand. He'd made it a point to always ask before his clothes came off.

She mirrored him, putting her bottle on the small bedside table. "Yep."

He stood and slowly unbuttoned his shirt, not wanting to scare her with his rapidly building lust.

Surprising him, she settled back to enjoy it, watching him with a steady gaze, as if she took in every moment to record for posterity.

"You planning to take your clothes off?" he asked, feeling a tinge of unexpected self-consciousness at her close study.

"Oh sure. But you first. This was your idea after all." Her voice was filled with a dare.

This was the part of Lynette he liked so much. She had the confidence of three women. As a wrangler she had to, or she'd be eaten for breakfast by the contestants. He grinned, then did a shimmy for a strip tease, turning his back to her and letting one arm of his shirt slide off one shoulder, half in jest and half deadly serious.

She gave a soft, "Oooh, nice."

Even though he'd had sex with plenty of women, he found this moment strangely intimate. Here was a woman he knew well, a friend he didn't want to lose. And he wanted her to enjoy every second of this, since he was pretty sure it would be their only time.

He didn't kid himself that this would be repeated. Their careers couldn't afford any scandals. And while he knew that he could weather any storm better than she due to the bullshit afforded to men, he also knew that if it got out that he'd abused his power and position with her, other female staff would avoid him. Sugar, for example, would quit in a blaze of glory.

So, he put his heart into this. He wanted to be remembered in her history books as the best one-night stand she'd ever had.

He let the shirt finally slide to the floor and turned back to her. "Your turn."

She swept off her t-shirt with little fanfare, and sat back in her bra, obviously not interested in returning the strip tease. But he wasn't disappointed, because it turned out she had fantastic breasts. Big without being huge. He longed to weigh them in his hands and took a step toward her to do just that. "Bra too," he suggested.

"You have to take something off first." She grinned.

He took off his right sock, dangling it between two fingers before flipping it over his shoulder onto the seat he'd vacated.

She laughed and mimicked him, tossing her sock onto the floor.

"Enough," he said, and resisting the urge to pounce, joined her on the bed, pulling her into a kiss.

Laughter faded quickly as their compatibility and hormones combined to leave them both gasping for air. He rolled her on top of him, so his hands had access to her bra hooks. It took a little fumbling but finally it came free. "Ah ha!" he celebrated.

"Good job," she said, her voice low and husky. "I was wondering if I was going to have to step in there."

"Always feel free to disrobe for me," he said. A small part of him acknowledged that this was the last time, the only time they'd be together. Sadness nipped at the moment, but he smashed it down, not wanting to ruin what time they had.

He slipped the bra off her shoulders and tossed it aside, then rolled her to her back so he could tease her nipples. "My God," he whispered, "you have beautiful breasts."

She arched backwards as he sucked first one, then the other, loving the feel of the weight under his hand just as he'd known he would. He'd never realized until now that he liked women with more up top.

"So perfect," he added, meaning every word.

She moaned and shifted beneath him, his cock riding between her thighs, brushing her sex through two layers of denim. "Pants," she gasped.

He stripped off his own, then helped her out of hers. But he left their underwear on, not wanting to rush something this good.

Their lips fed on each other, as his tongue explored her mouth. *My god, I want her. But not yet. Make this good.*

Her hips began to move below his, her wet sex seeping through both their underwear, heightening the sensation. "Is there a reason," she gasped.

He cut her off for another kiss, feeling like he was back in high school. It had been a long time since making out was so amazing.

"That we," they kissed some more.

Who knew that Lynette would be so good in bed? He wondered as he ran his cock over her clit, feeling her shiver every time he did it just right.

"Have our underwear on?" she asked.

"What?" He leaned away, trying to piece together her question.

"Underwear. Why is it still on?"

Her lips were swollen and deep rose red and he ran his tongue along them for a taste. She rewarded him with a shiver.

"Because if we take them off, we'll have sex."

"Aren't we here to have sex?" she asked, appearing truly confused.

He teased her with his cock again, enjoying her arch of pleasure and soft gasp, the sensation intense. To be on the same page with a woman, where her pleasure brought him intense satisfaction, made him feel like the king of the world. He set a rhythm, wondering if he could bring her to climax from the friction alone.

She shut her eyes tight and moaned, twisting away, but he caught her hips and kept her there, keeping slow and strong, following the buck of her hips to know the pace.

"Oh, oh," she whispered, fighting it.

"Come. Do it," he ordered, sweat rolling down his back as he tried to hold back from his own orgasm.

Her whole body went still and she grabbed his hips to stop his movement, too sensitive as she reached her climax. Shivers wracked her body, the convulsions making her arch and moan.

When she finally, finally, relaxed, he shed his underwear without losing his position and pulled aside her panties to slide inside her wet, warm depth.

"Perfect," he said, resting his forehead on hers, trying to not climax. *You have more control than this. Do not come. Do not.* He wanted to bring her to climax again, wanted to be first in her mind when she thought of sex.

She moved her hips under his, clenching his cock with her inside muscles.

"Don't," he panted.

"Why not?"

"Because I'll come."

"I thought that was the point?"

He groaned and pulled out a small amount, only to ram back home. It felt so. Damn. Good. Fuck it. He'd make it up to her later. "I promise I'll get you the next time."

"Next time?"

"Oh yeah." There would be a next time. He promised them both.

Her body joined his movement and then he raced to the finish line, his hips pistoning in and out, the feeling of her tight channel so damn good, he knew he'd never had better.

And then he came, the action rolling on and on as her sex tightened and released around him.

With the last bit of strength he possessed, he rolled off her, gathered her up and pulled her onto his chest. Then he fell into a deep, dreamless, amazing sleep.

CHAPTER EIGHT

*L*ynette had to pee. Badly. But she didn't want to destroy the moment of fantasy where she was cuddled into Hank, as if they were real lovers instead of a one-night stand.

It had been the best sex she'd ever had, even in her longest running relationships. She wasn't going to lie about that. Partly that had to do with the fact things had always been a tiny bit awkward between her and her partners, something she hadn't felt with Hank. He'd been her friend for a long time, and while she had no doubt she'd regret the hell out of this, she had to admit that their friendship had made the sex better. He'd been trying to make sure she came first, which any woman on the planet would agree was good stuff. But also he'd slowed down, made things last, communicated with her.

Surprisingly, she didn't regret they'd done this yet. She wasn't fool enough to think the end wasn't coming, but for now she was still floating on the fantastic feeling of being complete for the first time in so long.

Shutting her eyes, she shivered with the thought of his cock on her clit. So, so good.

"Cold?" he murmured, his eyes still closed.

"No, be right back." She tried to roll away but he came with her smushing her under him.

"Kiss first," he said, blinking open his deep green eyes.

She complied, the kiss leaving them both shivering. "Bathroom," she said, escaping the warm bed and walking across the ice-cold floor.

After taking care of business, she washed her hands, then tried to do something with her hair, which was snarled into a nest on the back of her head. Luckily her stick-straight hair didn't take another shape easily, and she was able to tame it with her fingers, since her brush was in the other room.

She touched her swollen, red lips, another bolt of need zooming through her. Man, the sex had been good. She sighed, brushed her teeth and opened the door, only to rear back as Hank stood filling the doorway.

"Sorry, I didn't mean to scare you." He grinned. "I was thinking we could take a shower and then go check on everything."

She looked at her wrist to find they'd burned through a chunk of their time already. She must have been out for longer than she'd thought.

"I'll soap your back," he offered, giving her that smile she thought was so hot. The one where his lips tilted in lazy amusement.

She should put distance between them, start the process of disentangling from whatever this was. Instead, she stepped back and invited him in.

He started the shower and captured her in a kiss. "Mmmm toothpaste. My favorite."

She laughed and he kissed her again, pushing her against the doorframe.

He held out a hand to test the water. Ice cold liquid splashed on her naked body. "Sorry," he said putting his body between hers and the icy spray.

"Takes a while to warm up."

"Of course it does," he grumbled, running his mouth lightly along the shell of her ear.

"Don't tell me you're having a negative moment," she said with a laugh.

"I know this place is a dump. I just don't want to spend my time thinking about it, when I can think about your amazing breasts instead." He picked her up and put her under the spray.

She screamed her protest, but instead of an ice bath as she expected, the temperature was perfect. "Oh," she moaned, and tipped her head into the water.

He soaped her up as promised, spending time making sure her chest was squeaky clean. She ate at his mouth as she pressed him against the sink. "Now how did this go?" she asked, trying to figure out the position that had started all the hormones racing between them days ago.

He turned off the water since it had cooled and reversed their positions, lifting her onto the ledge. Instead of going straight to sex again, he fell to one knee, parted the folds of her sex and ran his tongue from one end to the other, spending extra time on her clit.

She arched back, so sensitive from their earlier loving she could only gasp and moan.

He held her hips still as he laved once more over the bundle of nerves at the apex of her thighs. Bracing her hands on the back of the sink, she gave in to his demand and held still while his tongue drove her higher and higher. She had started halfway there, and the momentum of a fast climax rushed over her.

And then she was coming, the sensations so strong she only remained on the sink because he kept her there, holding her down, keeping her from sliding away from his mouth.

Contentment stole over her as he stood. Then he drove deep, hitting a wonderful place inside her that was raw and ready for more. "Please," she whispered, holding onto him for balance. She wanted this so badly, the press of his body and the thrill of him inside her.

The position robbed her ability to move, but he set the pace just right. "Almost, almost," she whispered.

Then she was falling, letting her head fall back onto the mirror as the convulsions wracked her body.

He stroked deep, then deeper still before his body shuddered its own release.

And for a wonderful moment, they rested there, with him still inside her and her legs still around his waist. She could stay like this forever, little quakes of pleasure still zinging through her.

Both their watches beeped, their agreed upon wake-up time suddenly upon them.

"Shit," he whispered, not moving.

"Damn," she agreed.

Back to the real world.

She didn't want to go.

She had to go. They had to finish filming so she could get the hell off this station and back to her life. Alone.

They disentangled themselves and with shaking hands, she dressed.

"I need to check the cameras," he said, but didn't leave, pulling on one shoe, then another.

She didn't look up as she put on a pair of boots, the soft leather usually bringing her considerable happiness. "Yeah," she said, feeling sadness nip at her.

This was the end. It had been worth it, she was pretty sure. She hoped.

"Hey," he said, materializing before her.

She glanced up and he kissed her. Slow, the passion smashed down now with only something sweet and deeper left. After a moment of hesitation, she returned it.

"See you in a few," he said and left.

As goodbye kisses went, it hadn't been bad.

Brushing her hair, she felt like a deflating balloon. Back to reality.

She tried applying some lip balm on her lips to cover their well-loved appearance, but it only highlighted how swollen they were. Throwing her hair hastily into a pony, she dragged herself into the kitchen for some coffee. She felt energized, keyed up, and exhausted all at once. Adding caffeine to the mix would possibly make things worse, but she needed something right now to get her back on track. Her mind kept tumbling over and over again with what happened last night. She'd slept with Hank Carson. She was both horrified and elated.

The small kitchen held a rudimentary set-up. They'd brought meals from Earth and had been warming them up. She heated some coffee and a breakfast sandwich. Both tasted old and worn out, like the room around her, the table she sat at sagging in the middle as if it had held something too heavy for too long.

Wolfing down much-needed food, she debated for a moment what signal it might send to Hank if she brought him coffee. In the past, she would have done it, but now bringing him a drink might signal some other intent. He might think she was pushing for a relationship.

The rules of what they'd had between them had been negotiated beforehand. They were simply getting the attraction out of their systems. Unfortunately, she had a rising suspicion that she'd only made things worse. He'd been better in bed than she'd been expecting. Most super-hot men spent the whole time you were with them at least partially thinking about themselves. But Hank had been an amazing lover, both caring and conscious of her pleasure.

Reaching a decision to do exactly what she would have done in the past, she pushed all the angsting away and warmed another round of coffee for herself, Russ, and Hank. They'd all brought each other coffee in the past. This was normal behavior. She couldn't debate every little action she made or she'd end up going crazy.

Taking the three mugs back to the command center, she found Russ still snoring loudly and Hank missing.

She put down the extra mugs and flipped through the few cameras they had running. Hank stood outside the suite doors talking to Mima. She turned up the sound, kicking Russ' foot to wake him. The cameraman stopped mid-snore, gasping for air as if she'd doused him in cold water.

"I'm telling you, that bitch did it," Mima screamed.

"What? What?" Russ yelled, jerking into a sitting position.

"Drama," she said, handing him a mug. "Drink this and make sure we're filming." Then she took her coffee and Hank's down one flight to join what was brewing into something bad. She could feel it.

When she rounded the corner, the fight stopped mid-sentence.

"Thanks," he said, reaching for the coffee with true appreciation in his tone.

"What's wrong?" she asked Mima.

"The hot water is totally gone. And that bitch," she pointed to Kyla's suite, "took it all."

Lynette avoided looking at Hank. "Huh. Okay." She took a sip of coffee trying to get her mind to work. Perhaps having sex in the shower hadn't been such a great idea after all.

Beside her, Hank carefully didn't meet her gaze.

The totally inappropriate urge to laugh bubbled up inside her. She let out a long breath and tried to think sad thoughts. "It wasn't Kyla's fault. I'm afraid we've been having problems with the water temperature for the last few hours. You'll have to do the best you can," she said, trying to keep any guilt from her voice. This was why the crew wasn't supposed to have affairs during filming. It created a butterfly effect of issues.

"I told you, biiiiiitch," Kyla's voice called from the other side of the door.

"Hey we don't have any hot water," Max said, sticking his mussed head from the door. He looked handsome, instead of bedraggled.

"We're working on it," she told him, shooing him back inside Emma's suite.

"Hi Max," Mima said, her voice full of sugar.

"Morning Mima," he said, winking, yesterday's fight seemingly forgiven. Then he ducked back inside.

Beside her, Mima gave a gusty sigh. "He's so amazing," she said, meaning it.

Lynette corralled Mima with an arm around her shoulders back into her suite. "Do the best you can with cold water. We should have more hot soon."

"I don't want to have my date without a shower."

She had a point. That did seem unfair.

"I'll see what I can do. But you look fabulous no matter what." Lynette meant it. All three women were tens out of ten on every metric. She hustled Mima into her suite.

"Can I at least have a cup of coffee?"

Feeling a bit sad, she handed Mima her mug, then pulled the door shut before the other woman could complain.

"Thanks for stepping in. Want mine?" Hank held out his own coffee as a replacement.

Normally she'd say no, but normally he wouldn't offer. She took it from him. "Thanks," she said to his shocked face, since it was apparent he hadn't really meant the offer. "I'm going to find Milton and figure out how long it takes to heat the water."

"Um," he said, staring at his coffee with deep sadness.

She walked away at a double clip before he did take backs.

Hank stood there, watching his morning java disappear, enjoying the view a little too much of Lynette's butt in her jeans. He'd never noticed it before. He found he liked curvy women. He'd had no idea of this preference. Or perhaps he only liked this curvy woman.

Last night had left him a bit disoriented. The sex had been amazing and he couldn't stop wondering why. Was it that Lynette was a totally different type of woman than his usual fare? Or was it—and he hoped to god this wasn't it—that she had been his friend first?

If the latter were true, then he was in trouble, because this went against his firm policy of keeping people at arm's length emotionally.

He sighed and went in search of more coffee.

In the kitchen, he found Jackson sitting at a sagging table, eating a bowl of what looked like mush. "Morning," he said.

Jackson grunted hello.

Hank warmed some food for himself, then ate while he fixed breakfast for the contestants.

Watching the other man, it occurred to him that Jackson would make a pretty good bachelor. Space engineer sounded like the perfect job to lure women onto the show and they could make a big deal about him coming back to Earth to find love.

Idly, Hank's mind cycled through some great promo copy. Just the man's picture would get the sponsors opening their checkbooks. "Have you considered TV?" he asked, eating a stale breakfast sandwich in quick, big bites.

"No," Jackson said, so final, Hank didn't feel any wiggle room.

A challenge stirred inside Hank, which made him grin. His favorite thing was winning reluctant people over to his crazy ideas. If he could talk his stuffy sister into becoming a contestant, he had the ability to talk anyone into anything. "We're out of hot water," he said, instead of going for the hard sell. He had three days left for that.

"Yep," Jackson said, taking another bite of his mushy porridge.

"It doesn't sound like you're surprised."

"I'm not. I had to pull the electricity from all non-essential items."

Irritation flashed through Hank. "Why didn't you tell us?" Before he and Lynette had sex in the last of it. "We can work around things if we know ahead of time."

"Take that up with Milton." Jackson threw his bowl into the recycler.

"I will." Hank pulled the food for the contestants out and arranged it on a tray. He'd deliver it, then go give Milton a piece of his mind.

"I don't think you realize how dire things are right now," Jackson said, then promptly walked out the door.

Hank was starting to regret his decision not to leave when the contestants arrived. Jackson had used the word dire. He didn't seem like a man prone to exaggeration. Besides, no hot water meant they were on their last legs as a show. Contestants had to look nice. That was what people tuned in to see, not a bunch of dirty malcontents.

Making a command decision, he decided to pull everyone down to the circus for a cocktail and start Max's next date earlier than he and Lynette had agreed.

CHAPTER NINE

*L*ynette found Milton in the circus having what looked like a large whiskey on the rocks with Alphie. This time, instead of being worried, she had some sympathy for him. If she stayed much longer on this space station, she'd join him and drink her troubles away.

"Rockin' Cosmos, Lynette?" Alphie asked hopefully as she walked down the steps, already reaching for his shaker.

"No." Alphie's specialty had made her too relaxed, too willing to let things happen without her participation.

"That's sad." Alphie's shoulders slumped even though his painted smile stayed in place. "I thought you liked my specialty?" His tone was just that side of accusing to make guilt spark.

Lynette shook her head at her instinctual urge to comfort the robot. He wasn't really hurt. He was programmed to mimic human emotions. "Milton," she said, causing the older man to start, sloshing brown liquid over the edge of his highball glass.

"Yes?" he asked, dread in the one word. As if perhaps he wished he'd never had them on his station.

She debated how to handle him. The defeat in his gaze had replaced the ringmaster bravado and jolly demeanor. Now, he had the squashed look of someone who was done fighting.

Not good. Not good at all.

She'd have to tread lightly. "The hot water seems to have run out."

Milton's Adam's apple visibly bobbed with a nervous swallow. "Uh well, yes. I explained earlier we had to give up some things to have the extra electricity you need to run the cameras."

"Actually, you didn't." He wasn't going to turn this back on her.

"Didn't what?"

"Explain." Lynette tamped down on her rising frustration, reminding herself she was going to be gentle. A new thought occurred to her. "I keep finding out new things have been turned off, but only when we need them. How about you give me a list instead of dripping things on us one by one?" She kept her voice non-confrontational when she wanted to grab his beige lapels and shake him. "What other amenities have we given up to keep the lights on?"

"Well, now, nothing too crucial," Milton hedged.

Alphie pepped up. "You should tell her about—"

Milton's hands fluttered in a hushing motion. "Now, now Alphie, let's not upset anyone."

"Tell me what?" Lynette asked Alphie. She had a sneaking suspicion she'd been talking to the wrong person all along.

"The rolling blackouts." He put a napkin before her. "Are you sure I can't get you anything?"

Suspecting he wouldn't give her information if she didn't order, she said, "I'll take an orange juice."

"Great choice!" He spun and zoomed along his track, happy as a clam, grabbing a box from the fridge. He plucked a glass from the rack and set it deftly on the napkin, pouring with a flourish. "Here you go! It's not as good as a Rockin' Cosmos, of course, but you should enjoy it." He waited expectantly and she realized she needed to take a sip.

She did so, the orange juice hitting her tired system with a spike of sugar and pleasure. "Best juice I've ever had," she said, and found that was true.

Alphie slapped a hand on his chest. "Thank you, Lynette. From you, that is a compliment I'll treasure."

"Now about those rolling blackouts," she prompted, dropping her voice and leaning forward on the bar as if she shared a confidence.

Alphie mimicked her, putting one elbow on the polished wood. "They'll start in an hour," he whispered.

Panic pulsed through her, but she kept her face friendly. "When you say blackout, what do you mean exactly." Surely they weren't losing power again. They couldn't film in the dark.

Milton added to her stress by putting his head in his hands, his shoulders drooping.

"We need to cycle down to only a couple rooms at any one time. To conserve energy."

Okay, that wasn't the end of the world. She could work with a couple rooms. "Will the cameras keep recording?"

Alphie shook his head, his perma-grin sending cross signals. "I'll have to take you down to one, I'm afraid. All these cameras are placing an unwelcome load on the system." He said it as if he was in charge of the station.

"When you say you have to take us down to one, are you telling me you're making the decisions on this, Alphie?"

"Milton asked me to help," Alphie said proudly.

"He did." She tipped her head to study Milton, who didn't meet her gaze. "Tell me you didn't put a robot in charge of the station, Milton."

"Well, Alphie isn't just any robot," Milton said. "And he can make things happen much faster than Jackson."

Behind her, boots rang on the stairs. She knew immediately who it was from the sound of the tread, but even more, she could feel Hank's energy. Her stomach tightened in anticipation, but she didn't let him distract her. She'd been doing way too much of that lately, and she had to stop. This conversation with Alphie was important. Her hormones could wait. An internal bell was ringing, warning of trouble and she needed to focus.

"You think that was wise?" Lynette asked, trying to hold down the panic.

"Is there a problem?" Hank asked from directly behind her.

Part of her thought *Hank is here. He'll figure it out.*

"They're going to start rolling blackouts in," she turned to Alphie who was the only person who would give her a straight answer, "how long?"

"Fifty-nine minutes," he said in his helpful voice.

"We'll be down to," she referenced Alphie again. "How many rooms?"

"Two plus the circus, of course."

"Of course." He wouldn't give up the power that ran his little fiefdom. "And we'll be down to one camera."

"That's not what was in the contract," Hank said, frustration riding his words.

"I'm afraid there is nothing I can do," Milton said, backing away from the pressure. "We need new parts. Until then, we'll have to limp along."

She believed him. They needed parts to run the station—parts they didn't have and couldn't get. Ergo, the station couldn't be fixed.

"Which two rooms do you want power in?" Alphie asked, as if it was a done deal. And she supposed it was.

"We can't do anything without our command center up and running. And we'll need the room we do interviews in," Hank said, surprising her with what felt like easy acceptance.

"What about the suite the couple stays in tonight?" she asked, pointing out the obvious.

"Didn't we bring candles?"

"Yes, but Hank." Why were they were bending over backwards to still try to make this work? This was a lost cause. She turned her back on Milton and Alphie. "I hate to say it, but this has gone too far. We need to leave."

Hank shook his head before she finished speaking. "We can speed up filming. I've already told the cast to be ready for it."

"Hank." She touched his arm, ignoring the frisson of goodness from the contact. "I know it's almost impossible for you to give up, but we need to walk away."

"We aren't defeated yet," he said, a Hank-like answer to every one of life's roadblocks. But now she wondered if his greatest strength isn't also his greatest weakness.

But enough was enough. "We can simulate being up here for the rest of the dates. We'll recreate the station in the studio. Make things look like we're still here."

"That will leave us with continuity issues. It won't be smooth and all those asshats online will have a field day pointing out how bumpy the filming is."

She tried another tact. "One camera won't give us what we need."

"We'll leave in thirty hours, cut it short by a couple days." Hank was trying to finesse this to the end.

It wasn't going to work. "Not this time. We'll miss shots and have to reshoot it all anyway. We can't stay here if they cut power like this. Contestants need showers to look their best. Thirty hours from now, everyone will look like shit." She knew that would be a huge consideration for Hank. She took the last gulp of her juice to keep silent, to give him time to come to the right conclusion.

He stalked over to the viewport and she let him go alone.

Come on. Don't dig in. Let go of this losing battle.

His shoulders slumped, and she knew she'd finally gotten through to him. "Okay. We leave now. Let's start packing."

"Oh, you can't leave," Alphie said, pouring her another orange juice even though she hadn't asked for one.

"What do you mean?" Goosebumps rose over her arms.

"We've been running the station by diverting the power from shuttle. I'm afraid you can't go anywhere."

CHAPTER TEN

*H*ank found himself trapped in place, his mind stuttering. They couldn't be stuck here. That couldn't be right. He'd finally decided that for once, he'd give up on the impossible and it turned out he couldn't leave anyway. The irony wasn't lost on him.

"You what?" Lynette asked, her voice level and calm. "Please tell me you aren't saying what I think you are."

"We took the power from the shuttle to run the station." Alphie wiped down the bar with sure, wide sweeps. "We had to get it from somewhere."

"Then give it back so we can leave." Lynette voice rose on the sentence, her building panic escaping.

Hank understood exactly what she was thinking. If they couldn't leave, they were well and truly fucked. They were going to die.

No, no, they weren't going to die. That was crazy.

From behind the bar, Alphie stood smiling. "Oh, we can't do that. I'll end up losing power again. That would be terrible."

She must have realized she was arguing with a robot. "Milton," she said, looking at the station owner.

"I'm afraid I have no idea how to move the power back into the shuttle." He opened his hands wide to show they were empty.

Hank had known from before he'd even left Earth that Milton was an idiot, had known the station owner was all show and little substance, but he'd gone ahead and come here anyway.

For the second time, he'd underestimated the dangers of space. He should have learned when he was on Mars. But no. He had to double down, come back up here and try again. Prove his idea was a winner. It had been pure hubris.

"Order him to put the power back to the shuttle, then we all get on it and go back to Earth." Lynette wasn't giving up.

"That would be terrible! Who would I serve drinks to?" Alphie asked in his peppy voice.

"You're worried about serving drinks?" she asked, incredulous.

Hank put a hand on her shoulder. "Are you telling us we're stuck here?" he asked, cutting to the chase.

Milton shrugged. "Well..." he hedged.

"Oh yes," Alphie said, as if that was the best thing in the world.

Hank realized Milton had given over control to a robot who wanted to serve them all drinks until they died. Which might be soon.

Behind him, Mima, Kyla, and Max came down the stairs trailed by Russ to start the cocktail hour as he'd requested. "Take care of filming. I'll be back," he told Lynette.

"Wait, what? You can't leave now."

He let the contestants finish coming down the stairs and met her gaze. "Keep filming. I'll be back. I promise."

"You're insane," she said softly, looking at him as if he were an alien.

"Have the contestants order drinks," he suggested, giving her the big eyes they used for hidden communication. He glanced quickly at the robot and back to Lynette. "You should order something as well."

She nodded slowly. "Okayyyyy. Everyone order drinks," she said to the cast.

"Great idea!" Alphie said, zooming over to start serving, their conversation forgotten. Or at least the robot was distracted, doing what he wanted to do above keeping them alive.

Hank took the stairs two at a time to the second floor, turning right into the off-limits section of station. He needed to find the one person who could help get them home. The only one here who knew the ins and outs of the station to the point he could wrestle back control from the robot. And the last person he wanted to ask for help.

A plan took shape in Hank's mind, one where the whole group snuck onto the shuttle and zipped away before the robot even noticed. That was the best way for them to be free. Because Milton had given over control to Alphie and wasn't going to take it back.

But when he made it to the control room, Jackson wasn't there. Hank roamed around the top floors of the station in growing panic, increasing his speed to a jog, dodging in and out of rooms marked Employees Only.

If they were stuck here, slowly using up the power on the shuttle, was it possible they would die? He found that a hard truth to swallow. He had to be wrong.

Finally, he located Jackson back in the sad little kitchen, eating a large meal of different dishes. "Help yourself," he said as Hank entered, pointing to several platters of what looked like warmed meat, cheese, vegetables, and a heap of mashed potatoes.

"We have a problem," Hank said, ignoring the food.

"You're just figuring that out, huh? Not the sharpest knife in the drawer, are you?"

Irritation flooded Hank, but he pushed it away. He needed Jackson on his side. "Alphie has taken over the ship."

"Yeah, I told Milton that was idiotic." He shrugged. "But like every shitty boss I've ever had, he didn't listen."

"What's going to happen if the shuttle runs out of power?"

"We'll all die a slow, cold death or maybe we'll die from the lack of oxygen first. I've been debating." Jackson pointed to the table. "You should have some of this. It will be the last hot meal we have in, oh, forever."

Hank reeled with the confirmation they were going to die up here, held hostage by a crazy robot. Lynette had been right. They should have left the moment the second shuttle had arrived. "There has to be some way around it. We need to take the power back and escape."

"I can't help you. Milton locked me out of the system, the asshole." He took a large bite of what looked like a steak dinner.

Hank closed his eyes and took a deep breath. He wasn't going to die up here. He was a fighter. He could make it out alive. "If I get you into the system, can you shift the power back to the shuttle?"

"I've already tried—"

"Can you?"

Jackson took another bite, tipping his head, the ponytail he'd put his long flowing locks into going back and forth. "Yeah. Maybe." He straightened. "Probably."

"I'll be back." Hank spun on one foot, then spun back, grabbed a dinner roll, split it open, popped on a piece of steak, and raced down the hall to find Russ.

Lynette timed the two women as they spooned water from a bowl into a cup as fast as they could to decide which contestant got the next date. "Five."

"Dammit," Mima wailed.

"Four."

Kyla spooned for all she was worth.

"Three."

Max held his breath beside her, but Lynette had no idea who he rooted for.

"Two."

Mima's efforts caused a large crash of water to hop from the bowl, flopping across the table to land at least partially in the cup.

"That's time! Spoons down."

"Cheater," Kyla snapped. "I saw that at the end."

"Takes one to know one."

"Bitch."

"Whore."

"Ladies, let's weigh the cups." Lynette brought out her scale and put it on the table. Then she zeroed it out and weighed Kyla's cup. "28.2."

"I think I won," Kyla whispered.

Mima's cup went on the scale. "28.3."

"I knew it," Mima yelled, breaking into a dance that involved popping her bootie up and down in Kyla's direction.

"Bitch," Kyla seethed.

"Last is always best," Lynette murmured to her as Russ recorded Mima's jubilation. "Remember, you'll be the last thing on his mind when he's making his decision."

Kyla visibly relaxed. "True. I'll make it worth his while." Her lips stretched into a shark smile.

Lynette wondered if Max had a chance. Kyla wouldn't be easy to say no to.

Lynette would have to race around setting up the candles throughout the suite to provide a romantic setting so they'd save the lights for another room. Why Hank wanted to do this, she didn't know, but he'd given her the trust-me look, so she would. What other choice did she have?

Max took Mima's hand and dropped a gallant kiss on it, then tucked her arm through his. They walked to the stairs. Lynette let Russ film them, then took off at a sprint to set up candles, hustling around the couple. "You guys stay in the hall while I set up." She broke into a run, which was awful and she hated it, but it had to be done. Grabbing the box from the command center marked candles, which she'd planned for the hot tub scene, she raced back to Mima's suite, noticing Russ was no longer in the hall when she ran by. "Two minutes guys. I'm setting up a surprise for you."

"Oooh, a surprise," Mima cooed, cuddling into Max.

Dumping the box on the bed, Lynette ripped it open and distributed candles as fast as she could. They'd need as much light as possible to film. After setting up every candle they had, she realized she didn't have a lighter. Taking the empty box with her, she speed walked back to the command center, telling Mima and Max she'd be back in one moment. Mima, who was provocatively lounging against the wall ignored her. Max gave her a wave, then returned his hand to where he caged Mima in, his body dipping closer.

Lynette saw the signs. If she didn't get them in a room and fed fast, they would be having sex against the wall in the hallway. She should run, but couldn't force her tired body any faster than a shuffle now.

When she returned to the command center, Russ and Hank were bent over the console doing something, but she had no time to ask what. Tossing things hither and thither, she finally located a lighter and dashed off.

One hundred wicks later, she escorted the couple inside and told them dinner would be served in a few moments.

Looking at her watch as she closed Mima's door, she saw she would have to warm dinner fast. Alphie was about to shut down the power. Breaking into a shuffle again, she raced to the kitchen.

She hoped Hank knew what he was doing and she wasn't racing around for everyone to die a long, awful death anyway. Her tombstone better not read *She Ran For Nothing*.

"So, you can do it?" Hank asked.

"Maybe," Russ said. "I have a backdoor I put in after my rights were taken away." He shrugged almost guiltily. "But I was only interested in looking around the system, not making updates."

Hank stared at him. "Why?"

"For fun."

Hank shook his head. He didn't need to understand Russ' brain. He just needed to get the power back to the shuttle. "Can you do it?"

"I'll need time. You'll have to take over filming."

Hank almost said there was no need to film, but then he reconsidered. If he could save their lives and get his filming done, his Emmy would be a done deal. "I'll grab a camera and get Lynette working on the interviews for the other contestants."

When he found her, Lynette was delivering dinner to Max and Mima, who didn't seem interested in eating. It had been years since he'd manned a camera. He didn't think he was any good at it, but he dutifully filmed the two eating.

"What are you doing?" Lynette whispered.

"Filming," he murmured back.

"Where is Russ?"

"Working on a project for me."

"Are you going to clue me in on what's going on here?"

"Let's put today's filming to bed, then we'll talk. You need to get the interviews done."

On the sofa, Mima gave a full-throated, sexy laugh as she fed Max grapes off her plate.

The lights went out. For a moment everyone froze even though the room was lit by candles. Then the running lights popped on in the hall. "I'd wondered if those would still work. I'll go get the other two women started," she said and left.

Watching Mima and Max as they cuddled, Hank was struck by how different his own night with Lynette had been. There had been none of this artifice, none of the well-rehearsed art of love. It had been two people, sweaty with need, with a goal of making the other person's experience as pleasurable as possible.

He found he preferred that.

As Max and Mima launched into a deep kiss, Hank's mind wandered away to how Russ was doing breaking into the computers. If they couldn't get the power restored to the shuttle, they were all doomed.

He found it almost impossible to believe he might die here. But what if he did? What if this was the end?

Well, if that was the case, he decided his last request would be to have Lynette one more time.

The realization made him pause and he almost dropped the camera, catching it in time to record Mima crawling into Max's lap. Hank drifted silently to the right to get a side shot of them, his mind barely registering the scene before him.

What did it mean that he wanted his last act to be having sex with Lynette?

It meant he had feelings for her that he wasn't facing.

Assuming they lived, he didn't want a relationship. Not with a woman who would demand—and deserve—his consistent time and attention. She'd want—and deserve—to have his full heart involved. Lynette would want a relationship that was real and deep. Hank had always avoided that at all costs.

It wasn't that he'd had bad relationships in his past. In fact, he'd never had strife in any of them. He preferred to be alone, in control of his schedule. He didn't like to come home and be obligated to eat a dinner that had been slaved over. He wanted to be able to go play pool at a moment's notice with his guy friends, take off randomly to fly to Paris for a party, or drink a beer watching a game if the mood struck him. Being tethered down sucked.

Yet he didn't want to sit around drinking beer in his last moments. He wanted to be with Lynette.

Mima pulled her shirt off, sexy slow, her body arching backwards to show off her perfect figure.

Hank captured the shot and dropped the camera by his side.

Once clothes came off, the contestants knew the cameras went dark. Literally. The last thing Hank needed was to have footage escape the cutting room floor and end up on some porn site. He wasn't going to be embroiled in some sort of scandal unless he'd personally orchestrated it.

Shutting the door as quietly as he could behind him, he walked down the hall, his mind back on Lynette.

Maybe, if they lived, he could see where things ended up. Try out dating her for real and see if it was possible. Lynette didn't strike him as someone who controlled her partner's every move.

They could keep it quiet. It's not like paparazzi ever followed either of them around. They were pretty much incognito to those outside of the TV industry.

Maybe, if they made it home which seemed like a growing impossibility, he would invite her to dinner. Just to see what could happen.

CHAPTER ELEVEN

*L*ynette stuffed Kyla back in her room, exhausted by the other woman's constant demands. Kyla felt like she'd been screwed by being chosen last, and maybe she had. Being last meant she was getting sloppy thirds. And with the timeframe running now at double time, Max was sure not to be at his best. Besides, after Mima was finished with him, Lynette was pretty sure he'd have the stamina of a wet noodle.

Walking toward to the circus, she stopped when she heard voices filtering up from below.

"You do realize that once the power in the shuttle is gone, we won't have any left at all?" Jackson's melodious voice said, the frustration evident. "We'll die out here."

"I'm working on getting the generators back on line," Alphie said in a peppy voice.

"And how are you going to do that, since you can't move from the bar?"

Lynette peered down to see Milton, Alphie, and Jackson huddled over the bar. They were whispering but a trick of the acoustics had their conversation coming right to her where she stood on the second floor, as if she was down there with them.

"I think you underestimate how much I can do from here."

It took a moment for Lynette to realize the last voice was Alphie speaking, because for once, his voice wasn't peppy. In fact, it sounded hard and serious. She shivered.

"I guess I have." Noise filtered up, the sound of heavy boots on the metal stairs. "I'm going to take a nap. You two can figure out how to save our lives, since Alphie has locked me out of the systems."

"Now Alphie, you shouldn't have done that," Milton chided.

"He was trying to put the power back into the shuttle. I caught him doing it." Alphie sounded pissed.

"Now, now," Milton said.

Lynette realized if she didn't move fast, Jackson would catch her coming out of the hall. Backing up, she stomped her feet extra hard, coming out of the contestant's hallway to go up the stairs. The conversation below stopped. Jackson reached the top of the steps as she entered the circus. He bowed, waving a hand for her to go before him on the stairs.

"Thank you." She climbed, feeling the odd itch on the back of her neck that said he was watching her butt. She supposed she should feel flattered Jackson was scoping her out. He was a fantastic looking man. Instead she felt nothing at all, because he wasn't Hank.

Man, she had it bad for her boss. She was so screwed. Wanting to stop thinking of that, she instead made idle chit-chat. "I put the contestants back in their rooms, but they aren't happy with the lighting situation."

"I've got some battery powered lanterns," he offered. "They won't last long, but it will help for a few hours."

Light would make a difference. "That would be great." She'd tell the contestants they were in charge of their own destiny and could run the lights as they saw fit. Once the battery was gone, it would be gone. That would placate them in the near term.

"This way," he said, leading her into a room to the left she hadn't been in before. He clicked on a flashlight as he entered. Pulling open a panel, he revealed several lanterns, handing her a couple.

"Thanks." She would return to the command center to find Hank, who owed her an explanation, then she'd drop these off.

Strangely, Jackson trailed behind her. She wanted to ask him why, but he skimmed against the wall as they circled the circus so no one below could see him pass.

Milton and Alphie still argued below, although their voices had dropped to a murmur she could no longer hear.

When they entered the command center, she found Russ hard at work. Hank paced back and forth like a caged animal.

"Jackson tagged along with me," she announced, unsure what to do about it. She wanted an explanation, but she hauled the space engineer in her wake like an unwanted appendage.

"What's the status on the access?" Jackson asked.

"He's in," Hank answered, not pausing his pacing.

Lynette could tell she was totally out of the loop. "In where?" She circled to look over Russ' shoulder but all she saw was a black screen with lines of numbers, letters, and symbols.

Hank raked his hands through his hair. "We're trying to take back the power, so we can leave on the shuttle."

Huh. They'd been busy. "Alphie and Milton are downstairs whispering. I think they're starting to suspect something is up." Everything clicked into place. She'd been running the show while they'd been in the systems trying to find them a way home.

Hank paused in his pacing. "Okay, let's assume you're right."

"She probably is. Alphie is pretty suspicious of me at the very least," Jackson said, moving to stand behind Russ next to her. "If he sees us in the system, he can lock us out again and we'll never get back in."

"If we need to distract Alphie, there is one sure fire way," she said.

Hank and Jackson stopped what they were doing to stare at her.

"Have people down there so he can fix them drinks." She put down the lanterns. "I'll grab Kyla and Emma and send them down."

"I'll go down and set up filming," Hank said. He turned to Jackson. "Can you take these to the shuttle while we're gone?"

She peered inside the small bag and found filming drives. "You're going to risk Alphie finding out you're loading the shuttle?" Hank wasn't thinking he could still have a show at the end of all this, was he? Surely, he wasn't that crazy?

"We need this footage."

"Screw the filming, Hank. What we need is to get out of here alive."

Hank had always gotten them out of every predicament. He'd gotten them out of every tight spot by brazening his way through, taking calculated chances. And it had always worked. This wasn't the time to risk their lives no matter how much he wanted that elusive Emmy.

"I need to go do some work on the shuttle anyway, reverse the power lines," Jackson said, forestalling an argument. "One of you can come with me and bring the box."

Lynette wasn't having any of his smoothing. "I want everyone to agree we're not going to die trying to get this show to Earth. People first. Filming last."

"I agree to that," Russ said from behind the monitor bank.

Jackson gave her a look which said clearly *Of course.*

She met Hank's gaze and held it, because he was the problem child when it came to this subject. "Agreed?"

His shoulders fell. "But—"

"I mean it Hank. Real life first. We can always simulate the station on Earth if we have to."

Reluctantly, he nodded, but not as if he meant it. "Agreed."

She had a bad feeling his need to finish the show would get them all dead. "I'll go unleash Emma and Kyla from their rooms," she said, leaving to make that happen, but wondering if all of this was for nothing.

Hank knew Lynette was right, but he had to not only get off the station alive but take all the video as well.

Maybe that was unrealistic and he'd have to abandon his plan, but at this point, he wasn't going to give up. This was supposed to be his chance for an Emmy. To finally win an award that was long overdue. He'd planned to already have one under his belt by now and it burned him up he hadn't checked that box.

Milton and Alphie huddled silently at the bar, as if he'd interrupted them. Milton's gray face and sweaty shirt spoke to the fact he was aware of the stakes at hand.

Hank tried to come across as casual as possible. He wasn't sure it would matter to Alphie, who might not understand the nuances, but he knew Milton was a smart enough guy to catch on if he didn't play this right. "Since we only have two rooms with power, I'm going to bring some contestants down here to film."

"That sounds great!" Alphie said happily, straightening and grabbing a cloth to wipe down the bar in preparation.

Milton said nothing, but when Hank came closer, he saw a bead of sweat traveled from his balding pate down his cheek.

Hank didn't react, even though it was a worrying sign. Milton appeared to be a man under intense pressure.

"Can I get you something?" Alphie asked, his voice hopeful.

"Water," Hank answered, knowing ordering would keep the robot's focus on the circus and not on what they were doing up in the command center.

He'd wanted to stay upstairs and personally direct Russ and Jackson, but he had to trust them to do their jobs. Besides, distracting Alphie and Milton was the key to this. If Alphie shut them down, they wouldn't get another chance. Not if Jackson was right about the dwindling power.

"I'd like to interview you both before the ladies come down." Hank put the camera on his shoulder.

"Me?" Alphie asked, blinking his eyes, the pleasure in his voice clear. While he might be a robot, he was also a sentient being, more complicated and scary than simple metal and synthetic skin.

"Of course. We'll splice your answers into this part of the season. You're a part of the station, one of the crew." Hank tried not to lay it on too thick.

The robot placed a napkin precisely square in front of him. "How exciting!"

"Alphie, how long have you been on Genesis III?"

"Oh, since the beginning." He poured water from a bottle into a tall glass. "Ice?"

Hank wondered how much electricity it took to run the bar. "No thanks. How long has that been?"

"3,644 weeks and two days, seven hours and three minutes."

Hank let the camera dip as he did the math. That had to mean that Alphie had been running for double the length of Hank's life. "That's a long time." He straightened the camera back again, knowing he'd blown the shot, but he couldn't do anything about that now.

"It was lonely after the people left, but I was able to keep the station running."

"I bet that was terrible." Hank wasn't acting. That would really be terrible. To be sentient, to have feelings, then to be abandoned. Not that the station owner could take Alphie back to Earth. His kind weren't allowed there. But surely someone had known what they were doing when they abandoned him like that.

"It was. Terrible. Every minute ticked by so slowly. Which is why you can't leave. You must stay."

Hank's stomach tightened ominously at the strength in Alphie's voice. "But even if we leave, more people will come. This is a hotel. And the show will bring even more visitors."

Alphie shook his head. "I'm afraid you're wrong. Milton told me he's done for, which I believe him to mean that he can no longer afford to run the station. The deal with the Middle Eastern prince who was to buy the station fell through. So, you see, there is no one left. Except the eight of you. Plenty of people needing drinks."

Hank switched the camera onto Milton. "Is Alphie right?" he asked, keeping his voice level, forcing the panic away. He needed to keep them talking and distracted. He wasn't going to flip out, even if he wanted to. Why had Milton warned Alphie they were going to abandon him again? That had been a large miscalculation.

"Well, maybe not, maybe not. If the show does okay, people might still come." Milton looked hopefully at Hank.

For the first time, Hank really understood what he was up against. Alphie had been alone for a long time, but it wasn't just that. He'd developed human feeling somewhere along the line and didn't want to be alone. And Milton had let the cat out of the bag. "The show will do amazing. We're going to win an Emmy."

Milton turned to Alphie. "See? Hank says it will be okay."

"I don't believe you." Alphie's tone dropped into a weird, dead cadence, more robot than happy person. "You want to leave me. Just like humans always do." Then he looked up to the top of the stairs as if he'd heard something Hank had missed. "Ladies!" he called. "Come have drinks!"

"Yay," Kyla shouted. "I thought we were going to be stuck in our dark holes-for-rooms forever."

Hank filmed them coming down the stairs, the happy chatter as the women snuggled up to the bar.

"What will you have?" Alphie asked, as if he hadn't just threatened to keep the cast here against their wills.

"What's your specialty?" Emma asked.

"Rockin' Cosmos. People go crazy for them," Alphie said.

"We'll both have one."

Hank wished he was upstairs, encouraging his team to figure out a way for them to escape. Because if they didn't get out now, he believed they'd be trapped here forever.

Jesus.

Kyla's huge presence filled the bar, as she flirted shamelessly with Alphie as he made the two blue drinks, painstakingly adding a real orange peel to the drink. Kyla and Emma clicked glasses and took deep swallows as if they were two best friends out on a BFF night.

"So, ladies," he said, trying to distract not only Alphie but himself with the interview. "How is your time on the station going?"

"It's been amazing," Emma cooed.

"For you. You already got to spend the night with Max." Kyla took another long swallow.

"This is so good," Emma told Alphie, as if to distract Kyla from her temper.

"Why thank you! I personally developed the recipe." Alphie zipped along the bar, then returned with peanuts in a bowl which he placed gently before them.

"Thanks, Alphie," Emma said, smiling at him.

"It's my pleasure. I am so honored to be with beautiful ladies like the two of you." Alphie gave them a half bow. The tone of his voice came across as sincere.

"You'll have your turn tomorrow," Emma told Kyla, circling back around to Max. "And it will be wonderful for you."

"I need a shower," Kyla told the camera.

"I can work on some sort of bathing water for you," he lied, fully intending to be gone by then.

Whatever was in the Rockin' Cosmos soon had even Emma laughing and talking a mile a minute. Hank filmed it all. Hoping and praying that Russ and Jackson were able to reroute the power.

From somewhere in the station, the whoop of an alarm sounded, making everyone at the bar jump. Hank wanted to put down the camera and race for the stairs. Instead, he kept filming.

With a sense of fatalistic dread, he knew they'd just had a setback.

CHAPTER TWELVE

"What just happened?" Lynette screamed over the blaring of the alarm to Jackson, chucking Hank's precious footage in a locker that had at one time held the candles.

The shuttle was lit by the two lanterns that had been slated for the contestants' rooms.

Jackson, who had dropped down into the crawlspace below the flooring to do the necessary work to prepare the shuttle, pulled himself up out of the hole. "This is the warning that the power's dropped too low. I need to get to the control room to shut it off. I'm finished here for now anyway." He grabbed one of the lanterns and left her standing there.

"Huh," she said to no one, looking at the open grate that appeared to be a giant trap in the middle of the floor. Should she cover it up? What if he needed to come back?

This was starting to suck. She picked up the other lantern and headed back to the command center to find Russ still clicking away. "How's it coming?"

"Almost done. When I set this off, we'll have to run our asses off to make it to the shuttle before countdown."

She wondered if it would make sense to move Max and Mima into the shuttle for the rest of their date? That would make it so she wouldn't have to wake them up or stop them as they had crazy sex.

But how to move them without tipping Alphie off?

Going past the circus wasn't an option since everyone below would see them, but hadn't Milton showed them stairs to the kitchen during their tour? She wondered if the doors below were locked? She went to check and found the way clear, the door opening right beside Mima's suite, marked Employees Only.

Making an executive decision, she knocked on Mima's door.

Max answered, looking like he'd just finished an MMA bout. His black hair, usually in perfect order, stuck out at every angle, his face that slack slate of the truly exhausted. His blue boxers sagged around his waist, his feet bare.

"You look like hell," she said before she could think better of it.

"Yeah, I know," he said dryly. "What do you need from me now?"

She raised an eyebrow. Max seemed about done with this game. She supposed he should have been careful what he wished for...

"Hi Lynette," Mima sing-songed, curving her body around Max, who flinched just a little. Her pink robe slipped off one naked shoulder.

"Hi Mima," she said, feeling an inappropriate giggle rise up. She valiantly fought it down. "We're going to restore power to your room, so I wanted to move you two to the shuttle temporarily while we get some work done in here."

Max perked up. "With our time almost over, maybe we should just end early?" A little hope crawled into his tone.

"Oh Maxy, you kidder." She kissed him, deep, with a promise. "I'll grab my bag!"

"Leave your stuff, Mima." The last thing they needed was the sound of rolling bag wheels moving along the halls. "We're fixing your room first and we have to be incognito."

Mima sighed. "How long will this take?"

"Only an hour or two." Lynette blocked the door. "No sound as we pass by the circus. I mean it. They are down having a drink with Alphie and I'm not having Kyla flip out that we gave you first dibs on a hot shower." Lynette went straight to the heart of what every person on this station wanted to ensure compliance.

"Oh, shower sex!" Mima squealed.

Max sighed.

"Not a sound." Toeing off her shoes, she tiptoed back to the circus, feeling the two of them following in her wake.

Below Kyla flirted with Alphie. "These are so dang good. What are they again?"

"Rockin' Cosmos," Alphie said in his happy voice.

Lynette put her finger to her mouth and didn't move until the two nodded. Careful to make no noise, she slid along the back wall, inching along to make sure no one could see her below. When they finally made it to the landing hall, she picked up the pace, wincing at the ice-cold floor.

"Watch the hole," she warned as they entered the shuttle. She put them in Max's old room just beyond the common area.

"We're staying in my room?" he asked, his voice full of suspicion. "One second, Mima, honey, I have to ask Lynette a rules question."

Mima nodded and roamed around, touching Max's extra clothes he'd left as backups.

Max took Lynette's arm, pulling her from the room, shutting the door behind him. "What is going on? And don't give me some bullshit that you're restoring power to Mima's room first. I'm not a total idiot."

Lynette knew Max was smart, but she'd been hoping he'd be too tired to be suspicious. "We are going to leave here the moment we can restore power to the shuttle. I wanted to make sure you were already on board so you didn't get accidentally left behind."

Max's eyes narrowed. "Why are we sneaking around?"

"Remember when the power went off when you were still on the shuttle?"

"Yeah."

"It turns out the station has been surviving off the shuttle's power for the last day. If we don't leave soon, there won't be enough power for us to make it back to Earth."

"And someone is blocking us?"

"Yes." In for a penny, in for a pound. Besides, Max wasn't scared. Even exhausted his gaze was sharp and his mind functioning.

"I want to help."

"I need you here, making sure Mima is safe. My job is to get everyone on board. When we leave, we'll move fast."

He sighed out his frustration. "You're treating me like I'm useless."

"You wanted an adventure and love and now you have it."

"Jesus."

"I need to know you're on board and safe, so there is no chance you'll be left behind. Because once we leave, no one is coming back. Ever." And she was never going into space again. Period.

The threat seemed to take the wind out of his sails a bit and he nodded. "I wish you'd left me with anyone else but Mima. I never thought I'd ever say this, but if I ever have sex again, it will be too soon."

"Talk to her instead."

"Talk? Mima doesn't talk."

"About her life goals. Her career. Her favorite fucking color. Tell her you have to get to know her. That the sex was great, but you need to bond." Sometimes she wondered if people were really this dense about their relationships. "Communicate now or suffer later." She pushed him back in his room and shut the door on his grumpy face.

Then she jogged back to the circus, shimmied along the back wall again, this time listening to Hank asking Milton what his plans were to upgrade the station.

Milton stumbled around, since obviously no upgrades were forthcoming.

She found Russ still typing. "How's it coming?"

"Almost there."

Jackson arrived. "We have to be out of here in one hour."

"If we don't, what happens?" she asked, almost not wanting to know.

"We won't have the power to leave."

Hank herded a drunk Kyla and a mostly drunk Emma up the stairs. The two women had become mellow and happy after their second Rockin' Cosmos, then slurred their words at the third. Emma had stopped drinking, but Kyla tossed hers back and within moments had staggered toward a sofa to lay down.

"Whoa now," he said, grabbing her arm. "Let's not do that." He pulled her up the stairs.

"Just need to sit down," she slurred.

"Emma, come with us."

Emma tottered to her feet. "I feel so sleepy."

"Alphie what was in the drinks?" Hank asked, wondering how three drinks could impact them so much when he'd seen the two of them each put away much more and not even wobble on their high heels.

"I always put a dash of happy juice on the top," Alphie said.

Hank could not let the two contestants fall asleep downstairs. If they made a run for the shuttle, they wouldn't be able to come back for them. And the last thing his ratings could take was leaving two of the women to die in space. That wasn't going to happen. No spin in the world would fix that. And besides, he wasn't that kind of asshole.

Luckily, they made it to the second floor before Kyla sat down.

He put his shoulder into her middle to fireman carry her the rest of the way.

"Woooo," she said, with a giggle.

Emma wandered off in the wrong direction and he had to jog to catch up.

"Uh oh, I feel sick," Kyla mumbled from his back.

"Emma this way." He dragged Emma along by the hand, hustling as fast as possible before Kyla threw up.

He almost made it.

"Great," he growled, putting them both in Emma's suite. "Emma look after her. I'll be right back." He had to get Lynette. Kyla couldn't be left unattended. "Okay?" He gave Emma a shake and she met his gaze blinking.

"Okay."

He raced double time up to the command center. "We have a situation."

"You don't say," Lynette said.

He pulled off his ruined shirt and tossed it into the corner. "Kyla is drunk."

"Uh huh." She studied his chest for a moment.

"Sick drunk."

"We should stash her on the ship, then, since she won't be able to run for it."

"Will that tip Alphie off?"

"I already moved Max and Mima."

"You did?" He wasn't sure if he was impressed or pissed. "We didn't agree to that."

"I made an executive decision."

He shoved aside his irritation. It was done. "We can't take them past the circus again. They're a mess."

"We'll need a distraction." She tapped one finger on her lips, thinking.

Russ tapped away at his keyboard.

"Where are we, Russ?" he asked, wondering if they even had time for stealth.

Russ didn't look up. "Don't speak to me."

Not wanting to stand here doing nothing, he met Lynette's gaze. "Okay we get Kyla up there first, since she's worse off."

"Who's looking after her?"

"Emma."

"Isn't she drunk, too?"

"Yeah, but not as much. She didn't have the third Rockin' Cosmos. I think Alphie drugged them."

"Where are you going?" she asked as he turned toward the circus.

"To get them."

"There is a back set of stairs this way."

He followed her, glad she'd remembered. He'd totally forgotten.

They found both women passed out when they reached Emma's room. Lynette rolled Emma onto her side—they'd have to return for her. Hank picked up Kyla and they went back up the back stairs and tiptoed past the circus, heading down the hall.

They entered the shuttle with only the waning light from the lantern Lynette carried. "Watch out. There is a hole in the middle of the floor."

"Do I want to know why?" He skirted it, glad for the light.

"Something Jackson was doing."

They went to Max's door and knocked. Max opened it immediately as if he'd been standing on the other side. "You," he said to Lynette.

Lynette bulldozed past him. "We need you two to look after Kyla."

"What's wrong with her?" Mima asked.

"She drank too much." Hank put her on Max's bed and made sure she was on her side.

"Why am I in charge of this?" Max was pissed.

"You asked to help. This is what I need." Lynette went to the door. "We'll be back with Emma. We think they've been drugged."

"Oh, poor things," Mima said and Hank could tell she meant it. Gone was the flirty femme fatale. In her place, was a caring human. Hank blinked.

"Let's go," Lynette said, pulling his arm.

It took them twenty minutes to repeat the process with Emma, leaving all three women smushed into Max's small room. They left him the lantern, which had almost faded down to nothing and returned to the command center to see how things were coming.

The clock was ticking down. Thirty minutes more, and it would be too late.

CHAPTER THIRTEEN

When Lynette and Hank arrived at the command center, they found Russ and Jackson arguing.

"What's wrong?" Hank asked, almost hating to hear. If these two couldn't figure out how to reroute the power, they were all going to die a slow death. A death they would see coming, as the power faded and the cold increased and the food and water froze. He stopped himself from going down the path of what they'd die of first—cold or lack of water. Or maybe they would simply suffocate.

But first he'd lure Lynette back into his bed. A bright spot in a bad reality. His mind's eye showed him the scene of them frosted over, cuddled together.

Holy smokes, that was a grim picture.

He wasn't going to let that happen. But he didn't like that he was having a fantasy about dying with her, his last wish to hold her.

"Jackson wants to take Milton with us," Russ said, blessedly distracting Hank from his thoughts.

"We aren't leaving without him." Jackson had the look of a man about to throw down the gauntlet, his golden locks a halo around his head.

Hank thought again that Jackson would be a fantastic bachelor with all his natural charisma. "While I have no problem taking Milton and would feel pretty bad if he wasn't with us when we left, I'm not sure of the logistics behind how to get him to the shuttle without Alphie realizing what we're doing." Although now that he thought of it, Hank knew he'd feel awful if they left the old man behind. It would be like a raw wound that would eat at him. Hank added Milton to his long list of problems.

"I told Jackson he's attached to Alphie's hip. There is no way to get him to the shuttle bay." Russ' voice was final.

"Well, we're going to have to figure a way." Jackson crossed his arms.

"What about the contestants? Our allegiance is to them first." Russ was ready to leave old Milton right at the bar.

"We've moved them all into the shuttle. As long as they stay there, they're ready to go." Lynette sat down on his bed, her shoulders ridged with tension.

He had the oddest desire to go sit next to her and pull her close. Comfort her. Hell, he could use a hug himself. *Focus, Carson!* "We'll have to lure him away."

"Don't tell me you agree?" Russ asked, incredulous.

"I do. No one gets left behind." He went to sit beside Lynette. She stiffened even more but he didn't take offense. They'd left things as a one-off. She didn't know he'd changed his mind.

"I can ask him to help me shut down the wings. We'd talked about doing that, but he hadn't wanted to let on that things were as bad as they were. We only shut down the bottom floor's north wing," Jackson said.

"Is that what the massive steel door was?" Lynette was relaxing beside Hank, the tension leaving her as she got used to his nearness.

He upped the ante by letting his arm rest against hers, enjoying the warmth of her through his shirt.

"Exactly. Each country added their own halls, building from the outside, before opening the hull after their sections were built. The doors allow safety if one section had a failure, but we can also shut down the power into those areas and save the drain. I can talk him into helping me, since we did the first one together. I warned him we should have done this much earlier, but he couldn't give up the dream that you would return to Earth to give the station wonderful reviews and the money would flow in."

Hank felt for Milton. How many times had Hank pulled something out at the last minute? He was the master of making it not only work, but blowing viewers' socks off in the process.

"So here is what I think we need to do. We lure Milton away to help with the doors. Once we have him up here, we run for the shuttle. Russ switches the power, we press the autopilot to return the ship, and we're gone."

"I love a simple plan," Russ said, sarcasm evident.

"You have a better one?"

"Nope."

"Jackson?" Hank asked, open to a better plan.

"I agree we'll have to make a dash for it."

"Lynette?" He met her gaze.

"This better work, Carson, or I'm going to be pissed at you."

"That would break my heart," he said, meaning it. He took her hand, twining their fingers, surprising her. But she didn't pull away. Not that he was planning to let her.

She blinked for a moment, squeezed his hand and shook her head, as if she couldn't figure him out. "What do I do to help?"

"Gather up the equipment and footage from today and get to the shuttle."

She groaned. "Good lord. You think you're going to get to Earth and still have a show, don't you?"

"You bet I do." He kissed her fingers, enjoying her surprise and stood. "Jackson, you want me to come with you to get Milton?"

"Yeah. Let's go."

"Are you ready?" he asked Russ, because if the power switch didn't work, they were totally screwed.

"The power isn't the part of this plan that won't work," Russ said, doom in his tone.

Hank took a deep breath. "Then let's get Milton."

Lynette took the last lantern and went back to the ship with the final box of equipment. She junked it into another locker next to the first, then sidled past the gaping hole in the floor.

She should cover that up, but what if Jackson left it open for a reason? She'd meant to ask him earlier but with everything they had going on, she'd forgotten. Too bad she didn't have one of those big yellow wet floor signs she could erect in front of it.

Raised voices drew her to Max's small room.

"I'm not sitting here in the dark. This is dumb," Mima declared.

"No one leaves," Max said, his tone final.

"I hate the dark," Kyla whined.

Lynette knocked softly so as not to startle anyone.

Max opened the door.

"Great job keeping everyone corralled inside," she told him.

"It was getting dicey. Glad you showed up."

"What's happening?" Emma asked.

"Yeah, what the hell is going on? You left us here, abandoned." Mima's flustered face flagged growing panic.

"We're leaving in the next twenty minutes." She put the lantern on the floor so they could all share it. She needed to decrease the panic before one of them ran screaming.

"I need my stuff from my room," Mima said and moving toward the door.

Lynette blocked her. "Stop, Mima. You can't leave."

"I need my stuff!" She zigged to go around.

Lynette sidestepped into her path. "We have a situation going on and you need to stay here."

"What kind of situation is it exactly?" Kyla asked.

"I'm not staying here for a single second," Mima declared, having reached the end of a rope even *Paradise* couldn't keep her holding onto.

"You aren't leaving." Lynette put all her authority into her voice. It didn't work.

"Out of my way." Mima punctuated the words with a shove that took Lynette by surprise.

Tripping on the lantern, Lynette crashed onto the bed, tangling into Emma.

"Owww," Emma cried.

Lynette tried to scramble up, finally finding purchase. "Wait Mima!"

But Mima was long gone.

Dashing into the next room, Lynette heard the crash as Mima tumbled into the open flooring. Lynette bent down to try to see if Mima was hurt, but could only hear her moving around below. "Are you okay? Max bring me the lantern."

The light illuminated one seriously pissed-off contestant. "What the hell is going on here? Was this some sort of trap?"

The gloves had to come off. "Anyone who leaves will end up staying on this station." She paused for effect. "Forever."

Everyone froze, including Mima who was already trying to climb out.

"What's going on?" Emma asked.

Max, at least, wasn't panicking.

"Nothing in your room is worth dying for." She told Mima. "There was some sort of maintenance issue right after the last shuttle arrived that drained the power."

"We're just hearing about this now?" Mima was probably covering her fear with outrage, but Lynette was getting to the end of the patience train with her.

"We didn't understand what had happened until the last few hours. We've been trying to free ourselves ever since."

"Why didn't you tell us?" Emma wasn't panicking either. Good.

"They were still trying to film the show," Max guessed.

It annoyed Lynette that he was right. "We're going to switch the power and leave in," she looked at the glowing dial of her watch, "thirteen minutes. So, let's everyone calm down, come back in the room with the light and pray like hell that we are successful."

Max offered Mima his hand and pulled her out of the hole without much effort.

"You're so strong," Mima said, smiling.

"Oh, please," Kyla said, rolling her eyes.

Lynette handed Emma the lantern and they all trooped back into Max's room. Lynette leaned against the door. She didn't care what she had to do. The contestants were staying put. Period.

CHAPTER FOURTEEN

*M*ilton didn't want to leave the bar. Hank suspected he was much drunker than he appeared, since he was swaying just a bit and his movements were overly precise. As he lifted the highball glass to his lips and took a small sip, his hand shook. "If there are two of you, why do you need me?"

"Hank and I can move the doors, but we need you to seal them. The sooner we shut down the wings, the sooner we can conserve power."

Alphie had stayed quiet, but his head was tipped to one side, as if he were considering the situation. "I think you're right, Jackson," he said in his peppy voice. "We need to seal off the wings. Then everyone can come to the circus and I can make them drinks!"

"Come on Milton," Hank said, trying to sound casual. "The sooner we do this, the sooner we'll be done."

Milton tossed back the end of his drink. "Fine. Although why you need me, I don't know."

"Let's start with the third floor." Jackson hustled the older man up the stairs, dragging him along by one arm. "We'll close off the one to the landing bay first."

Hank brought up the rear so Milton couldn't change his mind.

They made it to the top of the stairs and both grabbed one of Milton's arms to speed him up as they dashed down the hall, picking up into a run.

"What are you doing?" Alphie's voice called from below.

"What's happening?" Milton asked, stumbling, but they kept him upright, yanking to keep him on his feet.

"We're leaving," Jackson told him.

Milton tried to stop, but their momentum kept him moving. "We can't leave. This is my life's work."

"The station is finished, Milton." Jackson's disgust was evident.

Hank kept hauling the older man forward. This wasn't the time to have a hitch in the plan. Russ had set a timer to switch the power.

"It's not finished. This is a setback. Alphie has a plan to get the power back up and running. We just need to be patient."

"It's over, Milton. You can always start again if you still have your life."

"I want to stay!" Milton tried to stop again but they dragged him forward into the dark hole of the shuttle.

A door opened and light showed from Max's bedroom, illuminating the space just in time for them to avoid the hole.

"Stick him down there," Jackson advised. "He won't be able to pull himself out."

"I have to go back. Alphie needs me. He's going to save the station. He has a plan."

They lowered Milton into the hole. "You've got it all wrong. Alphie isn't going to save us."

"WHAT ARE YOU DOING?" Alphie asked over the loudspeaker in the landing bay.

The power to the shuttle went on and the lights in the landing bay went off.

This Hail Mary was going to work. Relief crashed over Hank. They were going to make it. He grabbed Lynette in a hug and gave her a huge kiss.

She stiffened, then melted into him, kissing him back. He wanted to pull her down onto the closest bed and rip off her clothes. Celebrate being alive.

Instead he set her aside. "Hold that thought," he said with a grin, then went to close the shuttle door, holding his palm over the button so when Russ joined them he could lock them in.

"The shuttle will leave in ten," a female voice purred over the speaker.

Outside in the landing bay, Alphie's voice still rang out. "YOU THINK YOU CAN LEAVE? NO ONE WILL EVER LEAVE AGAIN."

Russ came running awkwardly down the hall, his backpack making a clanging sound on every footfall.

"Nine," said the female voice. Seats with harnesses materialized out of the wall.

"Everyone strap in," Lynette ordered.

"Come on Russ," Hank called.

"Eight."

Russ dashed through the door.

Hank slapped the close button, the ramp retracting.

"Seven."

The cast scrambled into their seats, while Jackson leaned into the pit. "Grab my hand. You need to strap in."

Milton sat on the floor and sobbed. "It's all over."

"Come on Milton!" Jackson begged.

"Six."

Hank dropped into the hole and pulled a crying Milton into a standing position, hauling him toward Jackson.

"Five."

He shoved while Jackson pulled.

"WHAT DO YOU THINK YOU'RE DOING? YOU CAN'T LEAVE," Alphie screamed, this time from inside the shuttle.

"What the fuck?" Russ asked, going to a nearby console and typing furiously.

"Four."

Milton landed in a heap on the floor. Jackson dragged him into a seat and snapped his belts on.

"Three."

"That asshole is overriding my code. How is that possible?" Russ muttered.

A bad feeling stole over Hank. "Can you stop him?"

"Two."

"Trying." Russ typed like mad.

"Launch cancelled," the female voice purred.

"Bastard," Russ hissed, still furiously typing. "He hasn't taken the power back, but he's cancelled the launch."

"We're going to have to kill him," Jackson said, sounding defeated. "It's the only way to escape."

"He keeps overriding my code."

"You mean turn him off?" Hank asked. Why hadn't they done that before if there was a way?

"Alphie has no off switch. You have to separate his head from his body," Jackson said.

"Why didn't we do that before?" Because Hank had been thinking of the robot as a person.

"I just couldn't bring myself to hurt him. I'm still not sure I can." Jackson truly appeared to be conflicted.

Well, Hank didn't have the same attachment. He wasn't going to let Lynette and the contestants die if he could save them. "Don't leave without me," Hank ordered, slapping the door open.

Breaking into a run, he ripped the axe off the wall and headed for the circus. There was a piece of him that questioned what he was about to do. While Alphie wasn't human, he had feelings. But Hank wasn't going to die here. He'd try to talk Alphie into letting them go first, but he would need to do what must be done.

"What are you doing?" Alphie called up to him as he raced down the stairs.

"Let us go, Alphie. I don't want to hurt you, but I will if I have to." He circled until he reached the bottom.

"You will never leave. I won't let you," Alphie said in a robot voice.

"Let us go," Hank ordered, hefting the axe.

Alphie whirled, grabbed two highball glasses and threw them at Hank faster than a blink.

Hank barely ducked the first, but the second clocked him in the temple, making him stagger. Before he recovered, Alphie launched two more.

Hank dove behind a chair, glass breaking around him.

"Hank I have control," Russ said over the loudspeaker. "Come back."

A bottle of whiskey crashed beside him. "I can't. I'm pinned," he yelled, dabbing at the bleeding cut on his forehead.

"Wait, he's got control back," Russ announced.

Hank launched himself toward the bar. More glasses exploded as he crouched below the high top. The robot was so much faster than Hank would ever be.

"Come out from there, you coward!" Alphie screamed.

"We have control again," Jackson's voice said. "Whatever you're doing to distract him, it's working."

"I need help here." Hank popped up to see Alphie whirling to grab more glasses. He ducked down to avoid another volley and worked his way along the bar to where the robot stood, gripping the axe with both hands. "Alphie, we have to go home. We'll die if we stay here."

"I won't be alone again," the robot said. The anger and panic filling his words broke Hank's heart. But that didn't mean he'd stay here and die for him.

"Others will come." He inched closer.

"Liar," Alphie snarled.

From the top of the stairs, Lynette called, "Alphie, I know you're sad to be alone but we need to go home." She came down the stairs.

"You want to leave me." Alphie's voice came from right above him.

"We do." She finished the stairs and took a step toward them.

"Don't come closer," Hank said, not wanting her to get hurt.

"Are you bleeding?" She took another step.

Alphie threw two more glasses at her, hitting her left foot.

"Damn," she said, hopping backwards.

Hank had to do something, fast.

Lynette curled into a ball, trying to protect her head. Two more glasses hit her on her back.

Hank had to stop this before Lynette got hurt. Launching to his feet, he swung the axe as hard as he could, screaming in frustration.

Alphie's head separated from his body and bounced once on the bar, then dropped to the floor and bounced along to rest against one of the silver overstuffed chairs, the light still shining from the eyes. As he watched, it faded.

Alphie's body slumped forward, sparking.

"I have control again," Russ' voice said.

"If you don't get back now, there won't be power for us to return to Earth," Jackson said.

Wiping blood out of his eyes, Hank dropped the axe and pulled Lynette to her feet.

"My left foot," she said, wincing.

He lifted her into his arms. "Hold onto my neck. I'm going to run at the top of the stairs." Staggering a bit, he got them to the top and loped off to the shuttle.

It was only after he'd slammed the close button to the ramp and strapped both himself and Lynette in that Hank could take a deep breath. Alphie was no longer alive, but everyone else was. He had the footage for his surefire Emmy-winning show and most importantly, he would have the woman he wanted when he accepted that award by his side. And he didn't want to ever go into space again.

CHAPTER FIFTEEN

*L*ynette smiled at Sugar who'd brought her a beer at the wrap party. The party was up in the Hollywood Hills at one of their sponsor's homes, with a view of the city below and a posh, over-the-top set of furniture done almost entirely in unforgiving off-white.

They'd spent the last hour watching the blooper reel and it had been a doozy. Somehow, the camera in the circus had not only recorded the last moments on the station, Russ had also saved it onto the shuttle's computer before they'd left. He'd put the whole battle with Alphie to the soundtrack of an alien movie. When Hank had chopped off the robot's head, the cast clapped like mad.

She'd been on the lookout, but in the whole reel there hadn't been a hint that she and Hank had had a fling. She'd gotten away with it.

The thought didn't make her happy.

"That was a crazy adventure you guys had," Sugar said, grinning.

"You have no idea." Lynette took a long swallow of her drink.

"What happened to the fat guy in the beige suit?"

"Milton?"

Sugar took a deep swallow of her beer. "Yeah."

"He's gone back to his family in Nevada. Turns out his son owns a bordello there."

"A whorehouse?"

She shrugged. "Biggest in the state, from what I was told," she said, watching Hank talk to Russ across the room, both of them laughing. She missed him, but she'd better get used to it, since this was the end of their working relationship.

"Where do you think Hank will drag us to next?"

Nowhere, Lynette thought. Sadness flitted through her. "Lord only knows."

"Sugar, come quick," one of the lighting guys called.

"I'll be back," she said, disappearing into the recesses of the house.

Lynette slipped outside to enjoy the view. This was the end of her Bachelor days and she found herself mourning all the good times she'd had with Hank. They'd come back to Earth and scrambled to set up a fake station and reshoot some of the moments, adding in the hot tub scenes and famous singers, better food, and Kyla's night alone with Max.

In the end, Max had chosen Emma, which had pleased Lynette despite the fact she'd always had a firm rule not to pick sides. Emma adored him and for his part, Max seemed to like her. Lynette had wished them well and meant it.

Tomorrow, she had an interview set up with Montego Bay Hotties, a show that put twenty people into a house at an exotic location and kept them cooped up until they lost their minds for TV ratings. She found she wasn't as excited as she might once have been.

The sliding glass door opened and closed and Hank leaned on the railing beside her. She'd known it was him, of course. She could sense his movements with her eyes closed. It was so pathetic. Luckily, she only had to get through this goodbye conversation and she'd never have to worry about making a fool of herself again.

"Pretty view," he said, his arm almost touching hers.

"Yeah, it is."

He turned his back on it, leaning against the railing. "About us."

She grunted a half laugh. "There is no us, Hank."

"Yeah, there is." He gave her his lopsided grin she liked so much. "I've given you some space so we could finish filming, but since we're no longer on this project together…" He trailed off, seeming to struggle for words. Which was very un-Hank like.

"Yes?" It almost sounded like he was about to ask her on a date.

"I was wondering if I could take you to dinner?"

"Dinner?" she asked stupidly. The thought of a date with Hank Carson just didn't compute. They'd agreed to a one-night stand. That had been his rules, not hers.

"Yes. I pick you up, we go to a restaurant, order, drink wine, talk."

The glass door slid open and one of the key grips dashed to the rail and threw up over the side, bringing her a much-needed sense of reality. This would never work. An affair wasn't for the likes of her. She wanted more. The best thing to do here was run away.

"That's my cue to leave," she told Hank and pulled out her tablet to order a ride, tapping quickly so she didn't change her mind.

"Mind if I come with you?"

She stopped. "I thought you were inviting me to dinner?" Sure, she wasn't the type to settle for an affair, but the thought of having him again… No, no, that was dumb. She needed to stay strong.

"How about breakfast instead?"

"Breakfast?" She stared at him, wondering if she could walk away if she had him one last time.

"I think we should try. Just give it a shot. No one has to know. If it doesn't work, then we go our separate ways."

"I don't want something hidden."

"I don't either." He appeared sincere. "I'm asking you on a date, if I go home with you tonight or not."

Could she? Could she take a chance on him? Her heart was sure to be trampled if it didn't work. But what if it did?

"Just give us a week," he suggested, his smile bringing out a dimple in his cheek she hadn't even known he had.

God, she wanted to. So. Bad. But if they crashed and burned, it would hurt. Instead of saying no, she said, "You have two days to change my mind. And we're going to your house."

He raised a brow. "Why my house?"

"Because from what I've heard you don't bring women there. If I'm going to be in your life, I get all of you for two days."

He bowed. "My house, then."

They walked back through the party, skirting Sugar who was trying to remove a red wine stain from the off-white carpet, past Russ who was telling the production staff about his heroic battle for control with Alphie, out the door, and down the hill to the street below, where a car waited. No one looked their way, no one blinked an eye. They were always together, so their departure didn't cause a fuss.

She wasn't sure this was the right thing to do and spent the short ride debating the wisdom of this whole adventure. When he helped her out of the back, energy fizzed where their hands connected, reminding her how good it was to touch him.

She figured fuck it and went into Hank's tiny Cape. The house was on a side street with no view but had a cute patch of lawn out front and a swing on the wraparound porch. It was homier than she'd anticipated.

Hank locked the door behind them as she studied the cozy living room dominated by a dark leather sofa with accent pieces and art on the walls that tastefully gave a pop of color. "Did you decorate this yourself?" she asked, wondering if he'd had a girlfriend help him along the way.

"One of my sisters is a decorator," he said, and kissed her.

All her doubts, all her concerns fell away. His lips were still amazingly soft, teasing hers as the flutter of need grew inside her belly. She knew what was coming, knew how good he was in bed. Yes, she wanted him one more time, even if the next two days turned out to be a huge mistake.

Dragging his suit jacket off his shoulders, she encouraged him to pick up the pace. He helped her by shrugging it off and tossing it onto the leather sofa.

He scooped her up and carried her down the hall, upending them both onto his massive king-sized bed. In the dark, she couldn't see anything in the room and felt cheated. "Can we—"

He kissed her, distracting her for a moment as she kissed him back.

"Light," she managed, giving up on a full sentence.

He reached across and tapped something on the end table. A low, warm light filled the room.

"Perfect," she said.

"I love this dress," he murmured, working his lips along her neck.

"Hmmm." She'd worn it with him in mind. She figured the least she could do when seeing him for the last time was look as amazing as she could. And this dress did look amazing on her, hugging her waist and showcasing her breasts. She'd worn this dress as a tiny thumbing of her nose at Hank. She'd wanted him to miss what he'd had.

"The color is perfect on you."

She smiled. "Thanks."

He kissed her again. "But if you want it in one piece, it needs to come off you now."

She met his gaze. Seeing the fragile hold on his control, she laughed. "Is something wrong?" She presented her back to him so he could unzip her.

His fingers shook as he pulled the tab. Then he smoothed away the fabric, putting his mouth on her bare shoulder, leaving her only in her panties. "No bra," he breathed.

She shivered, chills racing along her skin. "No." It had been built in so the low back would show off the line of her spine.

He brushed the fabric down her body and tossed it onto a nearby chair. "Do you know how hard it was for me to act like nothing happened when we got back to Earth?"

"How hard?" she asked, needing to hear. Because her life had been a mess. If she hadn't been working day and night to finish the shoot, she would have gone into serious depressed mode. "Because it felt like you were avoiding me."

He laid back, tracing one finger along her breast. "I was totally avoiding you."

She knew she hadn't been imagining it. "Why?"

"Because I know what will happen to your reputation if the staff thinks we're screwing each other. I'm not that good of an actor to keep my feelings to myself."

He'd been protecting her.

Her heart lurched and with a start, she realized that her fate was sealed. She loved him. Dammit.

Instead of focusing on that, she kissed him, unbuttoning his shirt from the top as he unbuttoned from the bottom. It was a little bit of a scramble, but they had him down to boxers within moments. And then they were kissing again, flesh to flesh.

He felt so good, she couldn't stop running her hands along the smooth skin stretched over hard muscle. He rolled free to quickly shed his boxers and she did the same with her own panties.

Then he was above her again, hovering over her in a pushup, showcasing the wiry strength and lean muscles. "If we'd been stuck up there, I planned to ask you to sleep with me again."

"Yeah?" she asked, shivering from the anticipation of his entry as he slid back and forth over her sex, making sure they were both ready.

"It was my dying wish to have you."

She met his gaze. "I would have said yes."

He entered her in one slow movement sliding all the way to his hilt, stretching her so she bowed up and moaned his name.

They set the pace fast. No more talking as they both adjusted for maximum pleasure, with him driving deep inside in the perfect place she needed him to hit.

Pleasure built and built, then she was tumbling over, twirling into an orgasm most women only dreamed about.

Afterward, they lay there in a heap, the pleasure still shivering through them.

He curled around her and pulled the edge of the comforter over to shelter them from the cold. Warmth from his body filled her and she only felt a mild panic that she'd given her heart to a man who might not want it.

Hank woke slowly. He hadn't closed the blackout shades and the morning sun filled his room in a bright glow.

They'd woken a few times to have sex and he was well and truly sated.

That didn't mean he didn't want Lynette again. Maybe after breakfast. But one thing was for sure, this trial period wasn't going to be a trial. He was keeping her. For as long as she'd have him.

He sighed out a soft laugh at himself. How in the hell had he fallen in love with Lynette, when he was a confirmed bachelor, when he'd always wanted space from any women he dated?

But here he was. He'd not only agreed to giving her all of his life, he'd offered it up before she'd even asked.

"What?" she asked, awake beside him, smiling too.

"You're beautiful," he said. Laying in the sunbeam, she glowed. Her easy good looks would always draw his eye, but her mind was what had trapped him.

She blushed. "Thanks. You're pretty hot yourself."

He kissed her, then met her gaze again, tucking her hair behind one ear. "I'm in love with you, you know."

She blinked, obviously taken by surprise. "I—I didn't."

"It's true." He sat up. Well, he'd told her and she hadn't responded with her own vows of love. The die had been cast. He'd just have to convince her she loved him as much as he did her. He was good at that kind of thing. She wasn't going to resist him for long. "Want me to make you pancakes?"

"I—yes."

He grinned and found his boxers on the floor, then put them on.

She looked at her dress where it sat on the chair, then put on his white tux shirt, looking adorable.

He kissed her on the way by. "You get the bathroom first. I'll start the coffee."

After she disappeared, he wandered around his kitchen, mixing the batter and pouring two mugs. He took his into the bathroom as they switched, then came out to her setting his table, already looking like she belonged there. He leaned over her shoulder. "Ready for pancakes."

She nodded. "Are you sure?" she asked and he knew she asked about his declaration of love.

"I'm sure." He leaned a hip on the counter beside her. "You?"

"I've been sure."

"About what, specifically?" He wanted to make sure they were on the same page here.

"About loving you, specifically," she said, her tone deadly serious.

He grinned. "Okay. We start there."

"We start there," she agreed. She watched as he flipped the pancakes. "Working together would be tricky."

"Oh, we're working together," he said, not doubting their ability to make a great team.

"There are rules against the crew hooking up on set."

"We're not hooking up. We're together. That's different."

"The crew—"

"Will adjust." There would be some bitching, but they'd either like it or lump it. "I'm not losing my best wrangler just because of some stupid rule."

"Rules are there for a reason."

He divvied up the pancakes on two plates and handed her one, then led them to the two-seater table tucked against the box window. "Rules are there to stop volatile budding romances." He pointed to the two of them with his fork. "We're not volatile."

She took a bite and hummed with joy. "These are so good."

"My gramma's recipe." They both took a couple bites.

"It's going to cause drama," she warned.

"Not if we don't let it, it won't."

She ate in silence for a moment. "That's such a Hank Carson thing to say."

"Get used to it, babe. You're going to have Hank Carson for a long time if I have anything to do with it."

A slow smile slid across her lips. "Am I?"

"You bet." He wondered if he could talk her into moving in with him, then decided to save that for another day.

"So where do we film next? And it better not be in space," she asked, and he knew he had won her over when it came to working together. She took a bite of pancake, leaving a tiny bit of syrup on her lips.

"I think going into space twice checked the box. We need to move on." He grinned, loving the way she looked right in his kitchen. "I've found this amusement park."

She stopped chewing. "An amusement park?"

"Yep. It's called Atlantis."

"An amusement park."

"In a biosphere."

Her eyes narrowed as if she smelled a rat. "Biosphere?"

"It's under water."

She closed her eyes. "You're insane."

"And I know just the person to be the bachelor."

"I don't want to know."

"Jackson," he said, telling her anyway.

"The maintenance man from the space station?"

"Space Engineer." That title would make the ladies insane.

"This is a terrible idea."

"What's terrible about it?"

"You want to go underwater? Do you have a death wish?"

"The audience will love it. Fish in the background. Every shot will be gold."

"If you want water, why not an island. Like Antigua?"

"Boring. All islands are boring. They've been totally overdone."

"Then what about someplace super remote. Mongolia?"

"You know that's a high desert, right? There is like one bush per square mile." He took another bite of his pancakes. "Besides, I already signed the contract."

"We are so doomed," she whispered.

He leaned over and kissed the syrup away. "Actually, together we're unstoppable. Think about it. We've managed to make space work twice, and both times were a catastrophe."

A slow smile spread across her face. "I can't believe I'm saying this, but if anyone can make it work, it's you."

"There's my girl." He pulled her to her feet and spun her around, laughing. "Next stop, Atlantis."

"Atlantis," she agreed.

THE END

ABOUT THE AUTHOR

eigh Wyndfield lives in rural Virginia with her fat cat Ayra, two lovable rescue puppies, four chickens, and the best guy in the world. A city girl at heart, she's embracing the mysteries of growing things and watching deer race from hunters through her yard. Traveling and driving an ambulance round out her time. She writes romance fiction that is out of this world.

To learn more about Leigh Wyndfield, please visit https://leighwyndfield.com/contact.html#newsletter and join her newsletter list!